About the Author

Yugtha Y J was born in Mauritius in December 1999. Growing up, she discovered her love for young adult fiction and her passion for reading through Meg Cabot's Mediator Series. Ever since, she spent her free time getting engrossed in many other books. These gave her the opportunity to let her imagination run wild. She started creating and writing about her own fantasy worlds. By the time she was sixteen, she learnt to overcome her fears by turning them into fictional situations. She completed her first novel, *Aine,* shortly after she turned seventeen. Her motto; 'Feed your dreams with passion'.

Dear Valen,

I hope you get to learn about life just like Aine and make the most of it!

Yugtha

02/06/18.

AINE

Yugtha Y J

AINE

Olympia Publishers

London

www.olympiapublishers.com
OLYMPIA PAPERBACK EDITION

A CIP catalogue record for this title is
available from the British Library.

ISBN: 978-1-84897-014-8

This is a work of fiction.
Names, characters, places and incidents originate from the writer's
imagination. Any resemblance to actual persons, living or dead, is purely
coincidental.

First Published in 2018

Olympia Publishers
60 Cannon Street
London
EC4N 6NP

Printed in Great Britain

Dedication

To my mum and dad, who always push me to be a stronger and better version of myself.

Acknowledgments

For years, I have only dreamt of being a published author. There have been many instances when I started writing, but owing to my lack of self-confidence, I stopped. I was too scared of how people would react to the fruit of my imagination.

However, today, you are reading this. It means that a little girl's dream became a reality. I want to thank all those who contributed to *Aine*'s first success. Knowingly or unknowingly, you brought a lot to me, in terms of experience, maturity, encouragement and support. Thank you for making me believe in my words and in myself. All the small things mattered and I am very grateful.

I love you people immensely!

-Yugtha YJ

Prologue

I used to fear the day I was going to have to leave this material world. I used to believe that death was scary. Living seemed to be the most beautiful part of life.

We, human beings, are brought up to fear the uncertain and the unknown. We are used to clinging to what we seem to possess. We all know that we'll have to leave someday, it's inevitable. But not knowing when, how and what happens next creates the selfish creatures we are. Our nature makes us believe that what we see, is all there is to it. We tend to believe that the tangible and the visible are the only reality.

Why? Because of fear...

There's one thing I can agree to at such a stage though. It's true that we have to experience in order to be certain. Our mind requires what is visible and tangible to believe. Once we do, we realise that we were living in millions of lies. Lies which were meant to protect, restrain and contain us.

Chapter One

The agony only lasted a couple of minutes. Everything seemed dark and vague afterwards. I felt detached from my body while still being part of it. I felt like I was being pulled in two different directions; the human world begging me to stay alive and death as part of me was drifting into the peaceful darkness. It was a decision which I had got to make. I was just going with the flow, just like the current in a river. I was not making any efforts. I didn't want to struggle anymore. I have had enough of trying. All the questions I had about death were being answered. Death was a calm and gradual process. Life was different, probably in a bad way. I probably wanted to get away from it and discover the other world, if there was any. I've read about it many times. I just felt like it was time to finally face it.

If I had to compare, life resembled the rocky and steep road that did not cooperate with gravity. On that road, we just went too fast, unable to understand what was happening exactly, because we were too busy gripping the seats, praying we actually make it past the obstacles without any accident. Death was very different. It felt like the steady road we take for long drives. The one where we really got to admire the beauty of nature and everything around us; where the oxygen we breathe, felt pure and the temperature, perfect. That road seemed to be never ending. But that never bothered the one taking it because no one ever wants to be detached from it.

That was how it all seemed to me so far.

I heard the voices and the noises in the background. I heard people screaming, shouting and crying. Some were probably my friends or others who just felt the pain of seeing a major accident; I could not tell. I felt blind. I could not see anything occurring around my body. My eyes could not get away from the light I saw far in the distance. It was like a dot but it was shining so bright. I wondered if it was a star or heaven.

Do I have a good Karma? Or is it where judgements take place? Will I meet God? Does he really exist?

Those were the questions that ran through my mind. But I was not afraid. I was not the least bit scared. Little things used to scare me so bad. I wondered why not now. I could not bring my body to move and my eyes focussed on the light ahead. I heard a siren approaching. It was probably an ambulance or a police car, or both. I must have been soaking in my own blood like I had seen on television. My mind told me that I must probably have been looking like the human clay sculptures kids make in kindergartens; they had the basic shapes of a human body but they looked distorted and lifeless. My facial and physical features were probably wrongly angled and at this point, I didn't know how to react. It felt funny and at the same time awkward. Somehow, it felt normal not to care about the human world. Nothing mattered anymore. I was just waiting to discover what was going to become of my life or whether I would still have one or not.

I snapped from my thoughts on hearing a familiar voice next to me, pleading me not to go away. Nevyn. I felt his cold tears falling on my cheeks as if they were my own. I could not miss his voice out of thousands of other voices. He was the guy I used to love. But thinking about it, it was probably just an infatuation. We dated for one month before he broke up with me, crushing all the hopes and my heart along. I used to think he was different. Well, he was. No one ever broke me this bad. Thinking of him, had made me cry in front of hundreds of people, something I absolutely hated. Even though my delegation was nominated among the best delegations at the National Model United Nations' Conference, I could not enjoy. Why? Because I could not bear the sight of him flirting with the other girls. Seeing him constantly around that secretary hurt, but I was strong. I tried not to show it. I hid all the pain behind a smile; the same fake smile that was plastered on my face during the whole time.

I could not understand the reason as to why he was doing this in front of everyone. He told me that his feelings for me faded as time went by. He said that we could not be together anymore. He blamed it on his final exams and studies. He said that he had other priorities; that he had to fulfil his dreams and make his mother proud. I believed him and encouraged him in being successful even though it hurt. I did not try to convince him to stay. If he wanted to go, I'd let him go, even though my heart disagreed. But seeing him with the other girls, had started to remove the blindfold he tied around my eyes. He showed me his affection, but I could see him doing the same with the others. I wondered if he'd seen me around. I wondered if he had realised that I could see everything. If he knew he'd hurt me in doing so.

Or did he not care?

Probably the last one.

That night, I decided that I'd try to ignore him. He was hosting the after party with his friends, but I would not care and still have the time of my life. I partied and enjoyed with my friends. But when I saw him, it still hurt the same. So, I made myself emotionally numb. It was funny how not feeling, felt great! I could have fun and thinking about him did not do much. I saw the look on his face when he saw who I became. My guess; he could not recognise the version of me he used to know. That felt good as well. I wished that he would feel as confused and blank as he made me feel in one week. Just like I felt when he broke up. But, I never was one to wish anything bad for people and in that sense; I did not want him to feel the same. I was not trying to be a good person; I was selfish like any other human being. Part of me wanted revenge. I wanted him to feel what I went through. But part of me knew that it was useless, that I didn't want him to be sad and broken. I guess that it was simply my nature acting against my will.

That's when I realised that the best solution would be to act as selfish as he was. I had to concentrate on fulfilling my own dreams. That had to be my sole selfish love. It was something I had to do for me. I had to be the writer I wanted to be. I would create my own dream world. I'd teach people not to commit the same mistakes I did. The mistakes that could have led to my fall. But right now, I wanted to make the most out of the little time I had to enjoy. I could not afford thinking about all the bad he did. I wanted this to be the lifetime experience I've been dreading to experience. I would only care about myself because that was my current priority. However, in an attempt not to think, I felt a rush of memories. All the good and bad ones kept playing in my mind like the motion pictures. That's when I started feeling a panic attack. I could not stand being in such a crowd. It all felt too stuffy. The stress made breathing properly difficult. I had to get away before it got worse.

Starting to feel dizzy and sick, I made my way away from the partying crowd. On my way, I spotted Nevyn in the crowd. He was surrounded by so many girls. It was awkward how short they were. He seemed to be twice their height. It made me remember how we were close in height; probably a difference of five centimetres. I smiled at the memories but, he suddenly turned sideways and we locked eyes. The happy feeling lasted mere seconds. His face looked so innocent, but it's only when you learn to know him that you realise how much of a predator he actually was. He reminded me of the heartbreak and I quickly turned around, breaking the eye contact, hoping that he would not notice the tears filling in.

I felt sick again and I needed fresh air. I really wanted to forget and to be free of the bad memories. I had to get away. I felt eyes on me when I was near the door but didn't even bother to check who was there. It was a club, so it was probably security officers. I felt the hot tears spilling on my cheeks. I knew I was a mess. All I wanted was to forget this cruel world for a while. I was finally outside the club. It felt lonely but that was not enough. I was not far enough. I needed to be alone. I noticed a park on the other side of the main road. It felt lonely there; just what I needed. The trees would shelter me from the sight of others around. I would not be bothered by any other person there. The club had quite a large entrance, illuminated with fluorescent lighting. I hoped that no one would notice me and decide to follow. Hopefully, the music was loud enough to hide my sobs.

"Hey there! Stop!" I heard someone call out. That's when it hit me. We were not allowed to leave the club property without parents coming to fetch us because we were only minors. But that wouldn't stop me. The park is dark anyway. They would not notice me there. I'd come back when I felt like it. So, I just ran, hoping that they would not catch me. I didn't care about what they'd think. I just needed to make it outside and they wouldn't notice me in the park. They would probably not go on a hunt looking for me anyway. I would not stop running until I reached the park.

Running felt great and fun. The adrenaline rush in me was numbing again. I was not used to running so my body was starting to feel sore. I ran past the entrance and the gate. I only had to run past the main road. It seemed surprisingly big. My legs and my lungs were starting to give out. I was already out of breath but I still felt free. I was near to my current goal. But the moment was short lived.

The horn of a truck was all I heard, followed by an explosion of pain in my body. All the air got stuck in my throat as I felt my bones crack. Next, I was falling to the ground. I felt devoid of reactions. The few seconds felt like an eternity. I heard another crack as I hit the ground head first. The torment was numbing and I could not move nor utter a sound. It all occurred in a fraction of second. It was too much too take in such a short span of time. My body felt heavy and my mind could not respond. Understanding and realising, was a messed up combination. Then, everything blurred out.

Chapter Two

Moments later, I found myself completely cut from the world. The light which seemed to be only a small dot earlier was getting bigger and bigger. It seemed to be coming closer to me. It was approaching faster and suddenly, it felt too bright. I closed my eyes in an attempt to shelter them. I was nervous about what was going to happen. Slowly, I opened my eyes just a little bit, scanning for a source of brightness but when I could not find any, I opened my eyes. Part of me was disappointed as I was expecting something interesting to happen but part of me was just thankful that nothing bad happened.

"Aine?" I heard someone call in a masculine yet melodious voice.

It was coming from behind me. I could feel the nervousness rising. I felt my senses come back to me. I stood up and turned around. I was greeted by the definition of perfection. In front of me stood the most handsome boy I had ever seen. He had a slightly tanned skin tone, hazel eyes and slightly grown curly brown hair. It was cute how few strands of his hair would fall near his eyes. He was quite tall, about six feet probably. He was wearing some faded blue ripped jeans and a white V neckline T-shirt. The outfit fitted his well-built body perfectly.

"I thought that angels were supposed to wear loose white robes," I thought taking his presence and appearance in.

"I've never seen anyone wear loose white outfits around here actually." He told me casually.

I was shocked.

"Did he read my mind?" I wondered. *"Of course he might have, he looks like he could be an angel and I read that angels made use of magic. But if this is true, it means that he'll know everything that goes through my mind,"* I continued thinking.

My thoughts immediately went to how I thought he was handsome earlier and I felt my cheeks warm up on thinking that he might have read my mind. I looked at my feet, too embarrassed to face him.

"Great start Aine!" I thought to myself.

"In case you are wondering, no. I don't read minds."

I looked at him again, confused and obviously, shocked.

"Was that you?" I asked him all of a sudden. How could he not read minds yet, I hear him in my head.

"What if that was not him? But what's actually happening?" I asked myself.

"Yes, that was me and I apologise, I forgot to present myself. My name is Samhain."

"Hello, I'm Aine. Nice to meet you but, do you mean that it was you I heard in my head?"

"I know and yes, that was me."

"But how?"

"It's something normal here to be able to communicate through the mind. We only hear what others choose to share with us. You will learn about all of that gradually. Let's just concentrate on the most important things first."

"Okay, but tell me something- if I'm here, if I see you, does that mean I'm dead?"

"Your presence here means that you've left your human body somehow. We don't believe in death here. It is a term used in the human world to say that a spirit left his physical body. But the thing is, if you are here talking to me, it means you have a life. That's what I have read so far. But logic says that you can't be dead and have a life at the same time, can you?"

"Oh! So, now that I've left my human body, what's next? What do I do here?" I said, looking around me.

If I 'died', I didn't want to spend my life in this dark nowhere. I would probably just bore myself for eternity.

Samhain laughed. With his fingers still tucked in his front jean pockets, he leaned backwards slightly and raised his head a little. His curls bounced in doing so and I swear, he had the most perfect set of teeth. The look in his eyes seemed to be so pure and if I was not pursing my lips, I know that I'd be drooling. That was the most divine scene I had ever seen.

"Aine! You sound like such a young teenager!" I scolded myself mentally.

I looked at him, confused, expecting an answer.

"I'm sorry for my sudden behaviour," he said smiling, "But you should have seen that look on your face when you looked around. It was as if you felt horrified at the thought of staying here forever."

"You mean, is this where I'll have to stay forever?"

If I was not already dead, the shock he gave me would have killed me.

"How can I stay here forever? I thought there was supposed to be an afterlife and such supernatural things to do. How can I just stay in this place?" I tried to find the logic.

"Okay, I apologise for scaring you. Actually you don't have to stay in here." He announced, looking around him as if rescanning the room. "This is only one of the many transitional chambers. You can think of it as a portal or something. Usually, new coming souls find their way out as soon as they enter. However, at times, some souls like you, take time to separate from their material body. And you take more time here while feeling everything happening in the human world. Very often, it is due to something or someone you are attached to and you take time before finally letting go."

"You mean to say that I was not dead until I stopped hearing what was going on around me?"

"In human words, yes. This is what you are supposed to understand."

"So, now that I've left my human body and I'm completely in this place, how do I get out and where do I go next?"

"Getting out is pretty easy, flying upwards should get you to the door. That's where we need to go. Souls which come directly don't usually notice this place. But since you were taking more time than usual detaching from the human plane, I came to get you. Now if you'd please follow me."

He started flying to the top. That's when I realised,

"Samhain!" I shouted. "Wait! I can't fly."

Samhain turned around quickly. For the first time, I noticed his shocked expression but it disappeared as soon as it appeared. He flew back to my side and smiled.

"I forgot to teach you, sorry." He said in the sweetest voice. "Well, flying is quite easy. It's a mind trick. First close your eyes and imagine a feather. The feather is very light and it makes flying easy. Now, if you hold it and move it around, it will easily move in the direction you want it to be. To fly, all you have to do is imagine you are the feather and that you are the one moving the feather. The feather, that is you, will go in the direction you want to. You have to feel as light and in control. See! You are flying."

I opened my eyes and I could not believe it. I was flying! My feet were not touching the ground. I was standing in thin air with no ground beneath my feet. I could feel how staying around here was going to be fun.

"Aine," Samhain brought me out of my dreams, "Concentrate on going upwards, this is the only way to get out of here. Follow me."

He flew in front of me in the upward direction he told me to and I followed. I could notice light ahead and the closer we got, the bigger it became.

However, the light ahead was too bright. It started to hurt my eyes. I tried not to look at it and kept moving in its direction. We were very close to the other side, but suddenly, the light felt too bright for me to bear. I could not look at it anymore and my vision got blurry. I felt myself weaken.

"What if I can't make it to the other side?" I started to wonder.

I felt scared for the first time, since I died.

"What if I can't make it? Will I be stuck here? Is it because of the bad deeds I've committed?"

I tried looking for Samhain but I could not see him around anymore. Panic started to rise inside of me. Suddenly, my concentration broke and I started falling. The idea of being stuck in here scared me.

"Samhain!" I shouted mentally.

"Would my message reach him on the other side?"

I was wondering if that was going to be the end of me. If this is where my existence ended. I felt like crying but no tears would come out.

I felt a pair of arms hold my back and then I was being lifted upwards again.

"Aine, I'm here. Don't worry."

Samhain! He came back for me. Right then, I knew I could trust him. A friendship had started.

I wrapped my arms around his neck, holding on to him and together, we made it through the portal.

Chapter Three

"Welcome to the realm of Angels and Spirits," Samhain said, releasing me.

My eyes took a while to adjust to the brightness. When they finally did, I stood agape with wonder. This had to be the most beautiful place I'd ever seen. I slowly turned around observing my new environment. The portal we took was now closed. From the outside, it looked like a huge wooden door with golden symbols bordering it. The transitional chambers seemed to be found in a big cylindrical building. The walls were made of rock-like materials and they were covered in rows of golden engravings, just like the doors. It was strange how the symbols seemed to be attracting me. As I brought my hand closer and touched the engravings, Samhain shouted, "Aine! Don't!"

My fingers were already tracing the engravings. It was mesmerising how every time I would trace a symbol, it would glisten and shine. I turned around and looked at Samhain. If we were not already dead, I'd say he looked like he had seen a ghost. He regained his composure quickly and his expression changed as fast.

"What?" I asked remembering how he shouted 'don't'. I must have done something wrong. Now, this was weird. He seemed to be lost in his thoughts. I wished that mind reading had been one of the abilities I would have got.

"Samhain?" I asked gently, bringing him out of it. He shook his head in an attempt to push his thoughts away. His hair bounced lightly as he did and he pushed them back in one stroke and said,

"I forgot to tell you that we are not really allowed to touch the runes."

So, that's how they are called. *Runes*. I told myself memorising the name.

"Yes, they are one of the strongest forms of magic. Such spells and incantations are not really practiced anymore. They were only used in the enforcement and protection of the realm. Only few Chosen Ones have the ability to cast such spells." Samhain told me while admiring the runes himself.

"Who are those Chosen Ones? Are they some kind of angels?" It was funny how my curious nature followed me here.

"Once, there used to be a multitude of Angels. The first ranked angels who were the first to be created were the ones in charge. However, during the past era, many of them were destroyed protecting the realm and mankind from the dark creatures. The remaining angels had the ability to create very strong beings to ensure protection. They are also called Angels' Children. The angels blessed the purest souls back then before they were sent for their next lives. The prophecies predict that the Children will start coming back to the realm when the time for the new era is near. Some of them will come back stronger than others because they would have made it through all the steps and human experience would have made their soul stronger. But, some will come back weaker because of human mistakes which would have injured their souls."

I could not stop feeling amazed. This seemed to be pure fiction. Even the religious books do not mention such stories.

"When will that new era come?" I wanted to know more. I was new to all this and it just seemed surreal. I could not believe that I was living such a time. The bad guys will try to destroy the realm and they tried before. It was such a giant mess. I thought that Heaven- the realm was a place of peace and harmony, with undying flowers, trees and ghosts going around to look after their relatives on earth. Little did I know that it would be a battlefield for those who could not move on!

"No one really knows that, since the prophecies only say that the arrival of the Children will indicate that the time is near. That would only mean the realm must start preparing and training them for the coming war," he announced.

"But how will the angels know if the Children have come? How will they find them?"

"I've read that they are supposed to have special abilities which automatically differs them from the normal spirits. The books say that they will find their way to the angels when the time has come and the angels will do the rest. Now, don't you want to visit the place? I'll show you the best part, the library. Let's get going."

I followed him along one of the paths from the chambers. Everywhere was beautiful. The path was covered in white sand and fresh roses grew on each side. The environment felt natural and mystical. There were large garden like places separating the different paths. Samhain seemed to be so sure about the different way to go. I would probably get lost; there were no indications, just many different paths crossing each other. Perfection seemed to be a thing in the realm. Even the gardens seemed to be perfect. The grass looked clean and well-kept. Even the trees had no dying leaves. No flowers or leaves from the trees had fallen to the ground. It was so magical.

Noticing the gap between Samhain and me, I fastened my pace until I was right behind him.

"How do you remember which way to go? There are no indications anywhere."

"Do you remember I talked about one of the spells and incantations securing the place?"

"Yeah, what about them?"

"Well some similar spells were used to create those paths. There are not many buildings in the realm. The most important ones are the temple, the library, the transitional chambers, the healing chambers, the memory hall, the keeper's ground and the warding tower. The temple, the library and the memory hall are close to each other and in the same region. To its north, the keeper's ground and the healing chambers. Down the temple region, you've been there before, there's the transitional chambers. To its east, the warding tower where important ceremonies take place. It is said that when needed, one may find the secret passages. But that's only in the prophecies. They appear during the war for innocent beings apparently."

"But what about these paths?" I asked noticing he forgot to answer my question.

"Oh right! Well you only need to remember the regions and move in the main direction. The paths are a spell to confuse intruders if they ever manage to slip in the realm. Outsiders are never going to find their way around here. It's like the place knows who you are. You are your own key."

I felt like I would never stop feeling amazed in this place. But if there are so many protections, it must mean that the dark creatures must be pretty strong as well.

"By the way Aine, I have to inform you, the information I gave you comes from the books I've been reading. I have no idea to what extent they are true or if things have changed because I have never seen most of the buildings I told you about." Samhain said, running his hand in his hair.

"Oh okay! I guess that this has always been the same with books. You never know what's real and what's fiction!" I recalled from my own knowledge.

"But, I have to admit that I'm happy I found you. So far, I had never seen anyone around here and it was starting to drive me insane!"

I was quite surprised by Samhain's sudden confessions but I guess he really wanted to find a friend. Somehow, I could not help but laugh at his sudden over excitement. I followed him as he continued to show me around.

"Aine, look! This is the library." Samhain said smiling. "This is my favourite place to be in. But honestly, I think that that's because I did not have much to do," he admitted again.

I could not help feeling amazed. The structure itself was marvellous. I could not wait to see what it looked like from the inside. It was a white building with many golden encryptions above the door.

Samhain was already moving towards it. I was about to follow him when I felt a strong need to turn around. Not far from the library was a huge building. The biggest I have seen in that place. It was white and the walls were completely covered with the tiny golden runes. In front of it, was a set of stairs leading to a pair of closed white doors. The door itself seemed to be containing a lot. It was covered in several layers of golden runes. They were similar to those at the transitional chambers except that there were a lot I had never seen before.

"Samhain? What's this?" I asked not looking away.

"That's the temple. Not everyone has access to it."

I could feel Samhain's questioning gaze on me but I could not stop moving. I felt the temple pulling me. The vibes I was getting from it were sending waves of chill throughout my body. As I climbed the stairs, I noticed the round seal in the middle, joining the two doors. It had a pair of joined hands engraved on it. Standing at the door, I felt like this was where I needed to go. I felt Samhain's presence behind me. I could feel that he was curious about what was happening to me. I had the strong desire to feel more of the vibes. I reached for the door and placed my hand on the seal. It emitted a blinding golden light, causing our eyes to close. We heard the groaning hinges and the door opened.

Chapter Four

"Aine and Samhain! We have been waiting for you!" I opened my eyes to see a man, dressed in white and who seemed to be in his forties stepping closer to us. My eyes scanned my surrounding and it was nothing like I had ever seen before. We seemed to be standing in a high-tech room. There were holographic screens circling the room and each was being operated by some people. They all shared the same dressing style; sweatpants and plain T- shirts. The only exception was that the older looking people were dressed in white while the others either wore black or grey.

"What is this place?" I asked still looking around. My gaze fell on Samhain who seemed to be as shocked as I was. After all, we found what seems to be a computer room in the Realm of angels.

"This is the temple!" said the man standing in front of us.

I should not be so shocked, after all, I'm still new to being-"dead". But as for Samhain, I thought he knew everything about this place. Then, I remembered the part when he told me about only reading it in books. It made more sense that he would be as shocked as I am.

"Who are you and all these individuals? And how did this happen, I thought that the temple never opened to anyone!" Samhain finally added after a while.

"Well firstly, my name is Philip and I am one of those called Elders and these are the other warriors," Philip said gesturing to the younger looking people operating the screens.

"We are like you," he added, "Except from previous generations. We were once chosen to serve the Realm. Your presence here means that you have been chosen too."

"How is it possible that I am a Chosen? I've been here for a while now and it never opened for me!"

Since I had no knowledge about all of this except from what I learnt from Samhain, I could only listen to the ongoing discussion.

"Samhain, when you gave up on all hopes in the mortal world, it affected your soul. When you reached the Realm, you could not move on because you have a Chosen soul but you also could not enter the temple because your soul was injured. However, your genuine dedication in helping Aine cured you, and you could make it here with her."

Samhain turned to look at me. His gaze felt innocent and strong at the same time. I was trying to understand what it was he saw in me until Philip broke the silence.

"My children, I need to get back to my duties. Shanara will explain everything and show you around," he signaled to a girl who turned around. She seemed to be of our age. Her black hair was pulled in a ponytail and she was one of those wearing grey. She smiled and approached us.

"Shanara is a guide just like most of others here." Philip said. "Now, let us complete your initiation."

Philip joined his hands as if he was praying and whispered *crystallis.* Few seconds later, he opened his palms to reveal the plain black crystals. It was then that I noticed the similar crystals in the necklace of Philip and Shanara, except that Philip's was white while Shanara's was silvery grey. Crystals still in his hands, Philip whispered *initiatio electi.* One of the crystals flew towards me while the other flew towards Samhain. They circled around us for a while until they reached the center of our collarbones and lit up.

My crystal felt cold against my skin and I could feel that it had become an extension of my soul. It was as if it had a soul I could feel and both of our souls suddenly felt like one. I knew right away that its purpose was to lead me and protect me. I opened my eyes and realized that I closed them earlier. I touch my neck and felt the crystal. I felt a chain around my neck and realized that it was magic enough to create its own.

"You are now blessed by the power of the divine to serve your sacred purpose." Philip added while pressing a palm on each of our heads. "You may now fulfill your destiny!" He added before dematerializing.

I could not believe what had just taken place. But then I started wondering about everything he said.

"What could our sacred purpose be?" I thought thinking about Samhain and I.

Just then I heard his voice in my mind while we locked gaze.

"*I have no idea.*" I heard Samhain's voice.

"Follow me," Shanara said exiting the room.

"What you saw before entering the temple is what we call eternity garden. It is where you hardly ever see a soul. You should not leave the temple unless on a mission because you might get lost or show the path to dark creatures. Now, you must know that there are three levels of Chosen in the realm. All initiation begins as Warriors. This is the first level. It is like the neutral point. At the end of a cycle, you are reallocated according to what you are best at. You might then be either a Guide or an Elite Warrior. This is the second level like mine. After several cycles, some are chosen to be the Elders. Elders are in the third level. They counsel and advise the first and second levels. As you might have noticed Philip is in the third level and he also has extra powers as Elders are closer to the divine. Normally, after serving their purpose, the souls of Elders join the divine and protect the temple. Their bodies are then buried in the Garden of Elixir until it gives rise to a new tree of life. The prophecies also say that there might be Divine Chosen Ones. Their Crystals are different from that of the rest. But we don't know much about them as none appeared during the past hundreds of light years." Shanara stopped and breathed. "Okay, that was a lot to say." She added. "Do you have any questions?"

I was still trying to process all the information she gave when Samhain spoke.

"You said that the Divine Chosen ones have different crystals and I noticed that our crystals are different from yours and Philip's. What does that mean exactly?"

"Oh right, I missed that part! Well, your crystals indicate your level and your ability. Plain black ones like yours indicate first level. Second level crystals are either silvery grey or golden and black. Silvery grey crystals like mine are for guides like me while golden and black are for Elite Warriors. Elders however have white crystals which also indicate third and last level. Now, while first level only lasts less than one circle, second and third level lasts for as long as it takes for the soul to evolve. As for the Divine Chosen Ones, their crystals evolve differently."

Still reflecting on what she said, I added, "You said that the body of the elders are buried. But what exactly did you mean by that? I thought that our presence in this realm meant that we left our bodies in the mortal world!"

"This is because when you entered the temple and completed your initiation, you materialized again, like we all did. This means that as long as your body is concerned, it will mostly operate the same here. With time, you will learn to dematerialize again for some missions. To summarize it all, it means that you will still be tired after spending energy, you will still need sleep, and you will still sweat and need showers. For some occasions, you will need to dress up. The customs here are that everyone dress according to their levels and mostly in training wears. But if ever a mission requires you to go in the human world, you might dress as you want. The good thing is that you will not stink as a part of being pure. You will heal very fast and you will be very resistant to pain. However, certain weapons and injuries will hurt a lot and in some cases, death is possible," she added turning into another corridor.

"And where exactly does the soul go if one dies here?" Samhain added seriously.

"If all three levels have been completed, then to the divine but if not, it means that the soul was not completely ready and it will travel the spirit world until time has come for it to take a new birth on earth."

Shanara then stopped in front of some doors.

"These are the first level rooms. Your rooms have already been prepared. This one is for Aine," Shanara indicated the one of the left. "And the one next to it is Samhain's."

I went closer to my room to open it and stopped when I realized that there were no doorknobs. Confused, I turned to look at Shanara.

She laughed and added, "It's always the same reaction the first time. Well, here, unlike the human world, things are more exciting. To initiate your respective rooms, put your right hand on it."

We did as she said and we pressed on the doors with our right hand, golden runes appeared on the doors and disappeared as fast. Then, in golden letters, our names appeared at the top of the black doors.

"Original, right?" Shanara smiled.

Then I realized that she might be referring to the names. It really seemed easier to find our rooms.

"As from now, every time that you will need to open or close your room, you will just have to think about it and it will. No one else will be able to open your doors. You can now change into whatever black outfit you find suitable for training and take the time you need to look around and explore your rooms and your things. Time here works just like it used to back on Earth. I have some work to complete. Do your things and I will meet you outside your rooms in forty- five minutes." She gave us a last smile and walked away.

I turned to face Samhain and said, "Did you know about all of this?"

"I only knew what I told you earlier. I guess we have to hurry up now. I'll meet you in forty- five minutes." He answered before entering his room.

I stood still for a while registering whatever had been happening to me. I wonder what will happen next.

Finally, concentrating on the door, I thought, *open* and as expected, the door opened and I entered my new room.

Chapter Five

I could not believe it! My new room was no less than a luxury suite. On entering, I was greeted by an antique looking, wall length and wooden book shelf, and its matching reading space. There was a desk by the wall, with a candle stand, giving the cozy study place kind of look. The whole room had a black-carpeted flooring. Not far away was a wooden bed with black sheets and the same type of wooden night stand. This place had a thing for the candle lamp stand. It gave the whole room the antique ambiance. The room received its light only from the two windows behind the bed and the candles. From the window I could see a big garden with few pathways, but not the one I had seen on coming here. I noticed few people walking and wearing black. I guessed that they must be the other chosen ones. Opposite the bed were two big wooden chests. I went closer and opened them. One had different types of black outfits and the other had shoes. It was like a minimalist room, except for the big load of books. I saw a door on the other side of the room which I guessed was the bathroom. Shanara said that we were going to train, so, I took the first T- Shirt and Sweatpants. I added the first pair of black trainers and made my way for the bathroom.

As soon as I got ready, I looked at the clock near the desk. 14:35. I just hoped that I did not take too much time. As soon as I got out, I saw Samhain waiting next to my door. He must have heard the door because I noticed him snapping out of his thoughts.

"Cool, right?" He commented indicating our similar outfit.

That's when I realized that our clothes were identical. Same black t- shirt, sweatpants and trainers. The only difference would be in the sizes.

"I think that it's like uniform or something around here." I said remembering the people I saw earlier who were dressed in the same manner.

"Yeah! Don't you remember that Shanara said that earlier?"

"I thought she was referring to the colors," I said.

I looked around and there was no one. Shanara said she'd be here. I wondered if we were late and she left.

"Do you think that we are late?" I asked to ease my concern.

"Nopes." He answered casually, resting against the wall. "When I got in my room, it was two o'clock. And now," he glanced at his watch and added, "Shanara should be here in five minutes!"

For a moment, silence settled between us. All this is a lot to take in! A few hours ago, it was night time and I was sulking in a corner while watching my ex- boyfriend flirt at a party on Earth. Right after, I decided to have the run of my life, which ended it. Then I entered this sort of heaven and discovered that I get to be a warrior in my afterlife.

"What do you think we are up to?" I asked looking at Samhain.

Somehow, he seemed to be more knowledgeable about this, considering that he spent more time around here and in that library. I wonder what happened when he was alive that caused him to stick around. He had been weird ever since Philip talked about that part about this life.

"I don't know. I never heard or read about any of this. Those were never mentioned in any of the books." He said before getting back to thinking.

I don't even know how I should be reacting. I've been feeling kind of helpless ever since I *died*. I don't know what to expect so I have no idea about what's right and what's wrong.

"But whatever it is," Samhain added turning to me, "I think it's like getting a new chance at life, except that it is in another fictional world and we have to make sure not to make the silly mistakes we once did."

I don't know anything about his mistakes, but I know for sure that I've committed a lot and those should not be repeated again. It feels like here, anything related to 'human' refers to weakness and I should never be weak again.

"You are on time!" Shanara said approaching us. "It's awesome! Now, let's go."

We followed her back into the main corridor and kept going forward. There were several other small corridors like the one our rooms were in.

"All rooms on the right are for level one warriors and all rooms on the left are for level two. Elders do not reside in this part of the temple. It is possible that you might notice new room next to yours one day, it is because this place grows whenever needed to accommodate more Chosen ones. The amazing part is that you never notice it grew unless you walk and count the number of rooms. There are about sixty of level one so far. This place is similar to a school and dormitory in human terms. You will learn your schedules and learn whatever it is you need."

As we took some stairs to go down, Shanara kept on explaining the basics. Apparently, there are three hours of training per day and it is not basic physical training. We would also train to discover our special abilities. There is a training class starting in thirty minutes and after teaching, level two members needed to attend their respective duties. We walked through a gigantic garden. To me, it looked like a forest, except that it had light and it was very well maintained. After lots of walking, Shanara showed us the way to the dining room where we needed to be by eight o'clock.

"This is where all trainings will take place." Shanara said as we entered a hall on the other side of the garden.

It was a tall building with windows at the top. All around the hall were huge wooden chests. The walls were made of bricks and there were runes all over it. At the top were some writings in a language I did not understand. Soon after, other boys and girls entered the hall. They were all dressed like us; black crystals around their neck, black sweatpants, t-shirts and trainers. They were followed by three boys and two girls who seemed to be of Shanara's age and I could not help but notice their crystals. They were black and with golden twigs like design.

One of the boys approached us and said, "Shanara! What brings you here?"

I could not help but notice the big smile he had on this face. It was welcoming to see that they seemed to appreciate each other's company.

"Hey Nathan! Well I was showing the way to our new recruits. But I guess you can take it from here. We have lots of issues to solve in the board." Shanara tone suddenly changed to a serious one.

"Any new intrusion?" Nathan's concern kind of scared me. It felt like something bad was happening. He must have noticed my facial expression because before Shanara could answer, he said, "You know what, we will learn about it in the meeting anyway. I have to train our recruits here." He said looking at Samhain and me with a smile.

"Oh yes, of course!" Shanara turned to face us. "I have to go, Nathan is an Elite Warrior and he will train you. I guess I'll see you both later." And so, she left.

"Follow me." Nathan added while going towards the middle of the room where everyone was. "Guys, we have two new members as from today. This is…" He signaled me.

"Aine," I answered.

"And Samhain," Samhain said when Nathan signaled him.

"You guys are new here so everyone will help you to catch up. You will be as good in few days." Nathan told us and then turned towards all the others. "We'll be starting in ten minutes, everyone get your arrows and a bow."

Samhain and I followed the rest as we made our way to the chests to take the arrows and the bows.

I looked at Nathan as he joined the other Elite Warriors. I noticed their serious expression as they started discussing about something. I remembered the intrusion he mentioned earlier and wondered what it could be. I did not know much about this place but judging from their reactions, I knew for sure that whatever it is they were talking about could mean nothing good.

Chapter Six

We were in the training room to learn archery. The rest of the level one warriors had mastered it and were already practicing their shoots on the targets. Mihra, a level two and Elite Warrior was assisting Samhain and I while teaching us the basics.

"Archery is pretty simple once you find the technique. Or at least, it is easier than using swords which you will be learning very soon. Now let's get back to where we were. An archer must always be confident in his or her mind and posture. This is something you will always have to remember. Then, you always need to maintain the right position. Your feet must be shoulder width apart." She instructed us while showing us the right way to shoot. "Face the target. Nock the arrow using these three fingers." She said while she held her index finger above the arrow and her middle and ring finger below it. "This is called the Mediterranean draw or the 'split finger' style and it is the most advised position. The arrow should feel comfortable and as an extension of your arm. Next, raise and draw the bow, while maintaining confidence as you aim. Relax your fingers to prepare for shooting, as you move your hand back towards your shoulder and shoot!"

As she said so, her arrow left and in a split of a second it went straight into the Bull's Eye. She was an amazing shooter.

As soon as hers hit the target, another arrow hit the bull's eye on the target next to mine. When I turned around, I saw Samhain grinning next to me.

"Perfect!" Damien, another level two Elite Warrior shouted from the other side of the room.

"Yeah, Samhain, you are a naturally gifted archer." Mihra said as she came closer. "As from now on, you will attend practice twice. Archer practice with the other archers at ten o'clock and then back here for normal class at two- thirty."

I was happy that Samhain had found his ability. I, on the other hand, could not shoot quite right with an arrow and a bow. This went on during the whole class. Samhain tried helping every time but Nathan said that it was okay not to be good at something. He said that I would have to try other weapons to find where I excel.

"Okay everyone! We are done for today. Those who already found their abilities, be here again tomorrow at ten and as for the rest of you, we will meet again at two- thirty. Go do what you have to do and don't forget that diner will be served at eight and everyone must be on time. Before leaving put all of your weapons back into the chests. No training weapon out of this room." Zia informed everyone before going back to her fellow level two Elite Warriors. Another level two Elite Warrior entered the room and joined the others. I noticed his torn t-shirt and the black matter on his sword.

"Again?" Damien asked as the Elite Warrior entered the room.

"Yes, but it was not a very strong one." The latter answered.

"This is not what your outfit is saying!" Zia said sternly.

"He was just a bit angry because I killed his wife yesterday." He added grinning.

"Okay, let's hurry up! Today's meeting seems to be quite important. Callum wants all the level two and level three to be there." I heard Nathan said.

"What is it about?" Mihra added in a low tone.

"All he said was that 'things are changing'! Now, let's go!" Nathan added and they all left.

I noticed the speed in which they left. It was nearly as if they were not walking but instead flying.

"Hey! You are Aine, right?" I turned around and saw a blond girl talking to me.

"Yes and you are?" I asked.

"Kerah. You are new here so I thought that it is time you meet everyone. Leave all of this here and let's go." As she spoke, she took the gears, arrow and bow from me and she put them back into the chest. She then gestured for me to follow her and we made the way to the rest. There had to be around fifty warriors of level one in the room as some of them had already gone back for dinner. I noticed that Samhain was already getting along with everyone as he was bro- fisting some of the boys.

"Everyone, meet Aine." She said and it was followed by a couple of 'hi', 'hello' and 'welcome'.

"Hello everyone!" I added shyly.

"Aine, some of us are meeting tonight to have some fun. Do you want to tag along?" Another girl added. I noticed that she looked identical to the boy who was bro- fisting Samhain earlier.

"Yeah, sure!" I answered casually.

"What about you Samhain?" Kerah asked, turning to face Samhain.

"Yes, I'll come." He said. I admired how Samhain seemed to be natural with all of this. It was as if he had known them for ages.

"Great! So we'll go after dinner." Kerah told us before turning to the rest of the group. "Okay everyone, as usual, those free to come, we'll meet in the level one hall."

Gradually everyone exited the training room to go back to their respective rooms. I did not notice as Samhain left. He probably went earlier. Samhain was easily getting along with everyone. I was happy for him but at the same time it made me feel somewhat alone.

I entered my room and on opening my chest, I realized that most of my outfits were sweatpants, shorts and t-shirts. I took a t-shirt and a pair of shorts. This seemed to be more appropriate for nighttime than sweatpants. After I took a quick shower and changed, I started looking at the books on my shelf. They all had leather covers and a particular one caught my eyes. It had a dark level cover and red crystal designs circled around the edges. *Fortis Rubri – The Red Warriors.* Just when I was about to open it, I heard knocking on my door.

"Aine?" I recognized Samhain's voice.

I put the book down on my desk and ordered the door to open. Few seconds later, Samhain entered holding a black and golden bow and hanging on his shoulder was a bag containing arrows.

"Look at what I found in my room!" He held the bow for me to look at it.

"It's wonderful!" I answered. His bow looked amazing and it really seemed to suit him.

"I found it after showering. It was on my bed and there was a note along with it. All archers get one and I need to bring it for training tomorrow." I noticed his excitement as he spoke. He looked like a twelve-year-old on Christmas.

"You deserved it! You were amazing today! Even the Elite Warriors said so." Samhain really deserved all the praises he got. He was as good as the Elite Warriors at shooting arrows and that too on his first try without training.

"You have a bookshelf!" He announced.

"Yeah! Don't you?" I was quite surprised as to why he was asking me this. I thought that everyone's room originally had more or less the same interior.

"No, I don't! I had a shooting place instead but now I got the archery equipment." He said, taking a glance at my room. "I think," he added looking around again, "That our little 'extras' depend on what our ability is supposed to be. Mine was shooting but they did not know what exactly until I tried archery."

It all seemed kind of weird to me.

"What is mine then? Reading?" I wondered how that was supposed to help in a war or something.

"Maybe you have some super wisdom power or something." The way he said that made me think about the Marvel super heroes.

"I have no idea about what I'm supposed to do!" Suddenly, I looked at the clock near my desk and added, "We need to hurry, dinner is in five minutes and they all stress on being on time."

"Okay give me a second to keep this and we'll go." Samhain hurried to his room to keep his bow and arrows back while I waited for him outside.

In the meanwhile, I wondered about what my ability was supposed to be. Maybe it's really something related to books. After all, back on Earth I used to love reading. I can only wait to know what's going to happen.

"Ready?" Samhain asked on coming out to which I nodded.

"Let's go then!" He smiled.

We ran all the way down to the dining room but on my way, I could not stop wondering about what my purpose was around here.

Chapter Seven

When we reached the dining room, it was exactly eight. I was quite surprised to see no specific seating arrangements. After seeing the division in every section of the realm, I expected the dining room to be similar. According to the image I built, the three levels would have been differentiated here too. I expected a more luxurious service for the elders and seated like teachers in Hogwarts while level two Elite Warriors and Guides and level one Warriors had different tables.

On the other hand, the scene here was far from what I had imagined. There was a large area where the buffet was displayed. As for seating, there were different tables and everyone had the opportunity to choose their own seats.

"Aine! Samhain!" I heard someone call.

I did not take long to spot the voice among the crowd considering that the caller, also known as Kerah was also waving excitedly. I waved at her and with Samhain, I went to get my food. I was not feeling very hungry, so, I just went for some mushroom soup and made my way to the third table to sit with Kerah and some other warriors. Soon after, Samhain joined us with his plate filled with what seemed to be the whole menu.

Next to our small group, was another group of level two from which I recognized Damien and the other Elite warrior who entered the training room earlier from a fight. They were with another two Elite warriors and two guides. From the bits of conversation that I could gather, they were discussing the different techniques to *slaughter dark creatures?*

"So, as I was saying, are you guys ready for our little get-together?"

"Yeah," I answered. "But what exactly do we do there?"

"We are going to play a game and since today is about getting to know each other, we could try 'tell me how you'd –"" Kerah attempted to say but she got interrupted by another boy.

"So, you are the new archer joining us tomorrow, right?" He said addressing to Samhain.

"Yeah, I got in earlier today."

"Cool! Then you must have already obtained your gears and bow. I named mine Sephora." He announced proudly.

"Is it something everyone does here? I mean, the naming their weapons part?" I saw that in some movies and after all, on Earth people name their cars so, why not name weapons here!

"No, that's only Thomas' thing?" Kerah said. Then, pulling her tongue at Thomas, she added, "He is the only stupid one here!"

"You mean to say, the only original one here!" Thomas added, imitating some kind of 'grandeur'.

About an hour went by like this. It was fun being around everyone there. It had been around a day since I came and I already felt like I belonged here. Unlike how it was back on Earth people here had pleasant personalities. I enjoyed being here. I could already feel the unity that binds everyone.

Everyone altogether formed a single team to protect the Realm against whatever it was we were being trained to fight.

After dinner, Kerah and Thomas lead us to the Warrior's hall. We used our crystals as keys to unlock the door. There were already some of our fellow comrades waiting inside. They had already lit the fireplace, causing a cozy atmosphere in the room. The room was mostly a normal one- it had some couches and chairs around with few coffee tables. In the middle, was a huge navy-blue carpet, where everyone sat, forming a circle. What I could not recognize were the bronze statues standing in the corners, surrounding the room. All of them had real crystal, like ours, around their neck. The exception was that theirs were coloured; some red, some blue and for others, purple.

"Aine, come on! I can't do this without you." Thomas pleaded dramatically. His theatrical acts succeeded in making everyone laugh all the time.

"Beautiful, right?" A dark haired boy said next to me.

I felt a certain inclination towards the statues.

"They are the mighty warriors who once risked their lives to protect the Realm. They got killed in the previous wars. It is said that some of them had the direct protection of the Divine."

There were so many things to discover about the Realm and every time, it amazed me. I looked at the statues one last time before following the mysterious guy whose name I still did not know. I sat next to him as it was the only place left in the circle.

"Your attention ladies and gentlemen!" Thomas sung, theatrically. "Now that everyone is finally seated, I declare the game open."

After a while, I realized that Thomas was the funny and friendly guy around here.

He faced the dark-haired guy next to me and added, "Jake, my man! Will you please do the honors?"

Jake pulled a dagger from his waistband and spun it in the middle of the circle. It was similar to 'spin the bottle' except that it was mostly 'spin the dagger' here.

"Okay! Since today is about getting to know each other, we will play 'Tell me how you died'," Thomas continued.

The dagger kept spinning and we all gazed at it, eager to know who it would land on. We could feel the tension building in the room as the dagger gradually slowed down. Finally, it stopped and landed on a guy who I remembered was talking to Samhain earlier today.

"Aron you get to start." Kerah said excitedly.

"You may now speak!" Thomas dramatized.

"Okay. So, it was nothing very special. I was with my twin sister, Amanda," he gestured to a girl not far from him. "We were driving to a party. However, some stupid, drunk assholes were riding their bikes on the wrong lane and in an attempt not to kill them, I turned to the left but the car had already gone out of control. So, instead, our car went straight into an electricity pole and we both got killed. The end!"

"Quite the tragic hero you are!" His friend next to him exclaimed, smacking him on the back.

"Not too jealous, are you?" He answered doing a weird boy gesture.

I understood that our previous deaths are considered as funny experiences here and thus, the game continued.

The game went on for some time. Sarah died by drowning on an outing. Jeremy died from falling while climbing a coconut tree. As the game went on we discovered each other's death story. Finally, the dagger stopped and pointed towards Thomas.

"Well, my fellow warriors," he started, "Thomas, the Great died from playing a truth or dare – spin the bottle challenge. I had to recreate a scene from 'Now you see me 2, where the guy gets locked in a box and is thrown in the sea to try and come out. My friends had locked me into a wooden crate we found and put it in the lake. But unfortunately – or fortunately because being here is awesome-but yes, unfortunately, coming out seemed easy in the movie but not in real life. And so my friends, that's how Thomas the Great travelled from Earth to the Realm of Angels and Spirits."

Jake spun his dagger once more and it stopped to point in my direction.

"Darling Aine," Thomas joked, "How about you tell us your story."

Everyone faced me as I prepared to speak. Suddenly, I remembered my life back on Earth. I remembered the betrayal and the heart break. I remembered how people used to be cruel. Home never felt like home back then!

"Aine?" Jake called, snapping me out of my thoughts.

"Well," I began, "How I died is not as interesting as all of your stories. My team and I had just won at a competition and there was a party. It occurred few nights ago. For some reason, I could not enjoy and I was getting fed up. I wanted to go away, somewhere more peaceful probably. I started running to cross the road but a truck knocked me down and ended my journey there."

"This felt… intense!" Kerah commented.

"What? No, definitely not!" I added as a matter of fact. "Okay, let's continue." I said as I spun Jake's dagger.

It rotated on itself for a while and slowed down until it pointed at Jake.

"Mighty Jake!" Thomas joked. "Tell me how you died."

"On that night," Jake started, "My parents had gone out and left me in charge of my seven-year-old brother. Because of a phone call I had to leave him for few minutes while I went to my room. Suddenly, I heard an explosion sound coming from the kitchen. At first, I thought that he blew something in the microwave again. Ongoing there to check, I felt the heat and started seeing fire around. I called his name but I got no response. I entered the burning kitchen to look for him but instead, the gas Cylinder blew up and I found myself here."

Not realizing that everybody went totally silent, I asked slowly, "What happened to your little brother?"

Jake looked at me and as he talked, I could still see the pain in his eyes, "I don't know," he answered, his gaze defeated. "I never found out."

Before anyone else could speak, a piercing sound echoed in the room. It was soon followed by Philip's voice.

"Attention! Everybody is to report to the court room immediately. Level one Warriors are to use the main indoor pathways only. Level two Elite Warriors and Guides are to report in the court room first before getting back to duty. Those having weapons are to have them ready at any time. Be careful and stay on your guards. This is no light situation!"

The message kept of repeating and echoing all around the place. I watched as everyone started taking different paths. Jake was sliding his dagger back into his waistband.

"Jake?" I asked, anxious. "What's going on?"

"Seems like the war is starting!" He exclaimed peeking into the corridor. He turned to face me, taking my hand. "Come on," he said. "We have to hurry!"

Chapter Eight

We were running hand in hand, Jake leading me. I recognized some of the corridors but I had never seen the others. I had never been to the court room. I was still new to this world but, from what I had already gathered, I knew that this whole situation and the alerts had something to do with the intrusion the level two warriors were talking about. However, this particular knowledge didn't help. I still did not know what to expect. If this was as serious as it all seemed, then, I am currently a liability; a useless warrior with no ability.

We stopped in front of a door. Still holding my hand, Jake was tracing something around the handles. A pattern I could not understand but the design did amaze me. As he glided his fingers on the door, the golden runes glistened under his touch, similarly to how they did when I touched them for the first time near the transitional chambers. I guessed that whatever he was doing was completed as we heard the hinges groan and the door shone a golden light in between the space between the two doors. Before we could open it, I heard a screeching sound behind me. I guessed that Jake heard it as well because right then, he pulled me backwards and behind him as we exchanged positions. He was now in front as he faced the creature. I could not decipher its shape. It was gliding towards us like a moth. As it moved, it left a thick, oily and sticky like substance on the floor. It had a certain deformity as it moved, its body going along the change in direction. There was a round opening at the top of its body. A green substance was coming out of it. As it leaned backwards, Jake shouted, "Aine! Crouch down."

Shocked, I could not act straight away. I looked as the creature started coming back upwards.

"Now!" Jake added, bringing me out of the shock the horrible creature inflicted on me.

I crouched down instantly and watched as its mouth got enlarged and the green substance got sent in the direction where we were previously standing. The green substance landed on the wall and a foul odor got released as the wall melted at the contact.

Jake sent one of his daggers flying right into the creature's mouth. As he did, the creature opened its eyes. Four white eyes looked at us as it screeched and tentacles appeared all over its body. It moved towards us, whipping its tentacles in the air. Jake prepared to shoot another dagger but before he could, the creature hit him with one of the tentacles, sending him flying to the other side. Scared, I watched as his dagger fell in front of me and the creature turned around, moving towards Jake. The latter was lying wounded on the floor with nothing to protect him.

I felt a need to protect the guy who protected me earlier. Seeing him defenseless, hurt me. I took his dagger and looked at the monster who was about to hurt him. I noticed something on its back. A red corner, pulsing, camouflaged by the black substance forming the creature.

I had only one dagger; one chance to save Jake. This has got to be good. As I prepared to shoot, I closed my eyes, feeling connected to the dagger in my hand. I felt like I could do this. I trusted that the dagger, sent with my energy, would save Jake. Still closing my eyes, I concentrated on my one chance. *For Jake*, I thought and the dagger went flying towards the creature. I was scared and hopeful at the same time. I watched as the dagger I sent flew in the thin air. Just like I prayed, the dagger hit the creature on the red spot. The creature screeched as its heart burst opened and a black liquid spilled from it. I didn't notice some level two guides approach until they circled the creature. Concentrating with their eyes closed, it lifted from the ground and it got blocked with a silver looking bubble. The creature disintegrated in the bubble leaving a mass of the greenish liquid inside. Soon after it disappeared, the guides turned to face Jake. One of the guys went to Jake and made him levitate as he walked in another direction. I ran towards them to accompany Jake but I got stopped by a tall, blond guide.

"You did a good job out there," he commented looking at the spot where I shot the creature. "But, you cannot go with him. Not now."

I was going to ask why but he cut me, continuing, "Right now, Jake will be examined and cured. Then, he will need rest. You can visit him later but right now, you need to be in the court room."

"Sam," another guide, a girl, called from the group. "We will report to the council but you need to accompany the girl to the Court room. She will be safe there."

Sam nodded and the girl, followed by the other guides left.

I followed Sam to the already unlocked door.

"I hope you realize that you just found your ability, by the way!" He added, winking.

I smiled at the thought. It was still my first day in this kind of heaven and I saved a friend and found my ability at the same time.

He opened the door and all I saw was a small cubicle- like room. Still, Sam entered, his back facing the wall opposite to me. I went in and did the same. The door closed after me, revealing which looked like a set of 3D runes. Sam glided his finger diagonally across the runes, starting from one in the top left corner to the bottom right corner.

As if reading the confusion on my face, Sam explained, "This is a passcode to the court room."

We got lifted upwards and then we were surrounded by white smoke blocking the view. Seconds later, the smoke cleared and we were in a busy room.

"This is the court room." Sam told me, moving towards an elder one. "Follow me," he added.

I looked around and saw the level one warriors sitting on the floor while discussing. I noticed my friends as they watched me, equally as confused as I was for not joining them, while more white smoked appeared, revealing more level two elite warriors and guides bringing more level one and leading them to the others.

"Callum!" Sam called, greeting the elder as we approached. I did the same and greeted him with an inclination of the head too.

Callum and Sam shared an intense gaze and then they both turned to me.

"Who are your instructors?" Callum asked me.

"Nathan, Damien, Mih..." before I could finish saying Mihra and the remaining names of my instructors, Callum, turned towards a group of guides and warriors behind him who were discussing over some plans.

"Damien!" He called.

Damien looked in the direction and as soon as he identified the caller, he moved in our direction.

"Yes Callum," Damien answered, waiting for a reply.

"In such a time of need," Callum started talking turn to look at Damien and Sam until his gaze landed on me, "This can only be a great news." Then he faced Damien and added, "Your new trainee here has found her ability. She will be joining the shooters tomorrow. However, instead of ten, she will start at eight. You need to make sure that she catches up with the rest by ten. I don't think it will be hard though. If she can kill a Dramoniagus as a first timer, catching up as a shooter must be easy."

Then, he turned to me, "You will find what you need when you go back to your room. I need to let you know that what you did earlier shows your courage and an immense talent. I expect you to make me proud!" Callum smiled in a fatherly manner.

Smiling, I nodded at him.

"For now, go back and join your friends. We will meet again soon." He added before going back to join other elders.

I walked back to my friends and I got greeted by a warm embrace from Kerah.

"Aine!" She exclaimed. "Where were you? What happened? We were so worried." She added.

"I was with Ja—"

I was about to tell them about what happened to Jake and I when I got interrupted by the apparition of all the level two warriors into the room. They all moved to where the elders were. I noticed Nathan among the crowd of Elite warriors. Some had torn clothes and scars while most of them were only slightly dirtied by what I recognized as the black substance of the Dramoniagus. They were followed by the apparition of the other Guides who seemed to be in the similar state.

"Level one Warriors," Callum started, "It is now safe for you to go back to your rooms. What happened today was no simulation. This only signifies that the war is coming soon. You are expected to be on your guards and to take your training seriously. Training is maintained for tomorrow. You may now exit."

My fellow level one warriors started leaving. I watched as Callum got back to talking to some other elders and some level two guides and warriors. I spotted Sam talking to two other Elite Warriors further from the rest of them.

"Come on, Aine," Kerah said moving forward.

"You go ahead, I'll see you later. I need to talk to someone." I said, going out of the crowd of level one and towards Sam.

"Sam," I called when I was behind him.

He excused himself from the two other warriors and turned to me.

"Yes Aine?"

"I was wondering when I could meet Jake. You know, after he got wounded and taken away. I didn't see him since."

"You could meet him now, but he must be sleeping and you need rest too, So, I suggest you go sleep too. You can then meet him at the infirmary first thing in the morning."

"Alright, I'll see him tomorrow. Goodnight," I said as I started leaving.

Suddenly, remembering I was new, I turned around and called, "Sam?"

"Yeah?" He turned to face me again.

"Umm –" I started, "Where is the infirmary?" I asked.

"Oh yeah!" He exclaimed, remembering I was new. "You know what," he continued, "I'll lead you there tomorrow. Be ready by six- thirty!" He added smiling before going back to the other level two guides.

I followed the other level one warriors and walked faster than usual until I was next to Samhain.

"Hey!" He said looking at me.

I smiled and we walked to our rooms in silence. When we were close to our rooms, he added, "You look exhausted! You should get some sleep."

"You are right," I said yawning. "Good night then!" I added before entering my room.

On entering my room, I saw the gears, daggers and a letter on my bed.

I opened it and read the exact words Callum told me earlier in the Court room. For the first time, I felt the need to fight for something. I knew he trusted me and all I wondered was whether I would be able to make it up to his expectations.

"I expect you to make me proud," he said.

Chapter Nine

"How did this happen?" I heard someone asking in a hushed tone.

"I heard that it was an accident."

I saw the two ladies talking in a corner. I was in a crowd of people in what seemed to be the living room at home. Most of the people were dressed in white. All of the facial expressions were mostly similar; sad or sympathetic. I wondered what was going on.

"Excuse me!" I said, hoping that some people would move and let me see what happened in my own house. No one seemed to hear me as none of the people attempted to move.

I decided to go the hard way, pushing through the crowd like people do at concerts. I tried to make my way, pushing the two men in front of me apart. I felt pushed by gravity in front as I stumbled losing my balance. However, none of them moved. They seemed as disturbed as when a cold breeze blows.

Shocked, I continued trying to push through the people in front of me but the same thing occurred until I was in front. There was a body on the floor, dressed in a white suit on a flower bed. A funeral. Without paying much attention to whose body it was, I continue moving until I found myself in another room. People were coming and going looking sorry. They were there to express their sympathies to *my family?*

I saw my mom talking to my aunt.

"She texted me a bit before it occurred, telling me that their team had won. I was too busy to reply then. I wish I did. I'll never get the chance to congratulate her."

"Mom, no!" I said, crying. "I am sorry for hurting you this way."

Right then, I remembered everything. Less than a day ago I died. My soul went to the Realm of Angels and Spirits and on entering the Temple, I materialized again and found a new life as a warrior. Earlier I fought a Dramoniagus and found my ability. I got my own set of dagger and soon after I went to bed.

So, this is a dream! But, I can't be dreaming about my own funeral. I need to wake up! I really need to wake up now...

I woke up crying and sweating. I quickly looked around, confirming my surrounding. I was in my room at the Realm. The sun was starting to rise outside. I looked at the clock near the desk. It read five in the morning. I tried going back to sleep but I was too disturbed by my dream to relax.

I decided to occupy myself until it was time to meet Sam. I took a quick shower and then went to the bookshelf to find a book to entertain me. My gaze landed on the book I left on my desk the previous day. *Fortis Rubri – The Red Warriors.*

Just like back on Earth, I got engrossed in my book here as well. According to my new book, the Fortis Rubri or the Red Warriors are a type of what Shanara described as the Divine Chosen Ones earlier. They were the blessed children with powers from God. As I read, I discovered one of the powers all of them had; the power to summon fire from incantations and runes. Since I was surrounded by candles, I took a turned off one and tried summoning fire. Using my new dagger, I carved the fire rune, a geometrical design looking similar to an S, on the candle. Then, eyes closed, I concentrated, pinching the top thread on the candle and chanted the incantation. *Circa aërem ignis a me da mihi.* As I did so, I felt heat travel from my heart, along my arm to the tip of my fingers on the candle. I opened my eyes and as I released the hold on the candle, the candle ignited.

"Shit!" I exclaimed loudly, clearly shocked at the result.

Suddenly, I heard knocking on the door. I looked at the time. Six- thirty. I commanded the door to open while blowing out the flame on the candle and putting it back on its holder. As Sam entered, I closed the book and set it back on my desk.

"Good morning Aine," Sam greeted me. Then, looking at my desk, he said, "Do you like the daggers? I was the one to get them delivered to you last night."

"Yes, I love them." I looked at the gears and the daggers I put on my desk before sleeping. "But I still can't figure out how to wear these." I said holding the gears.

"Lift your shirt," Sam said taking the bigger gear.

Shocked, I looked him straight in the eyes.

Realizing what he just said, he added, "I mean, this goes around your ribcage. I'll help you wear it." For the first time in the Realm, I noticed someone blushing and that too, a deep red blush.

I started laughing at the awkwardness of the situation and soon after, Sam joined me, complaining about how embarrassing this was.

After a small class of learning about how to tighten the gears around my ribcage and above my ankles, I followed Sam out of my room and we walked all the way to another part of the temple.

"This is the infirmary," Sam said, opening the door.

As we entered, I saw Jake talking to an elderly lady.

"Jane, I'm completely fine now, I promise," he insisted.

"I believe you but you still need to drink this," Jane said holding a glass of greenish liquid.

"But, it looks disgusting," Jake said, peeking into the glass before adding, "And it stinks!"

"It does not taste so bad though. It's as good as pomegranate juice," Jane said trying to convince him.

Hesitantly, Jake took the glass and swallowed its content.

"Yuck," he commented, wiping his mouth and giving the glass back to Jane. "I thought I could trust you!" He dramatized.

"Good boy!" Jane praised patting him on the head like a puppy. "As a reward, let me inform you that there's a beautiful girl coming." She signaled me to come forward.

As I walked towards Jake, he turned around and exclaimed, "Aine!"

"Hey," I said approaching him, "How are you?"

"I'm great," he said smiling.

I looked at the cuts on his arm. I could only imagine what worse injuries were hiding under his shirt.

As if reading my mind, Jake lifted his shirt slightly, looking at the bruises and cuts and showing me at the same time. "Oh, don't worry! These are mild injuries, they will probably disappear by this evening."

As Jake was taking back his daggers, Sam appeared next to me and addressed to Jake. "To compensate your lost dagger," Sam started and I knew he was referring to the dagger I killed the Dramoniagus with, "I was told to bring you this."

Sam took something out of his back pocket and gave it to Jake. Jake unwrapped the piece of black material and revealed a new shining dagger with a coper handle.

"This is so cool!" Jake exclaimed, grinning. "Thank you." He said to Sam.

Sam then excused himself to get back to work. I spent some time talking to Jake at the infirmary about everything that occurred the previous night, carefully skipping my dream. I was not sure if it was normal yet.

When it was close to eight, Jake accompanied me to the training room for my early shoot practice. He helped Damien in training me to catch up with the other shooters. Catching up was not that hard. I discovered that I had a gift for shooting daggers.

When it was time for the normal class, I discovered that we were only ten to have a thing for daggers, with me being the only girl. Damien, engaged us on a virtual simulation while teaching us how to kill a Dramoniagus and the other demonic creatures; names I could not memorize yet.

I could shoot a Dramoniagus straight, but some of the other creatures could teleport faster than the moth like creature. Killing the other demonic creatures would require more real training and for that we would need to train on the battlefield with the other level two warriors.

Damien announced that we would leave for the edge instead of going to our other evening class. From what I understood, the edge is where there were recent openings from where demonic creatures could easily enter the Realm. For now, the edge was only a deserted land at the far end of the Realm after the Calila forest.

The class was over earlier on that day, giving us two hours to prepare for the training, or secret mission as I call it, before reporting in the court room at one.

I followed Jake to the kitchen for some extra 'supplies,' as he referred to it. However, I was too stressed about our coming training to really concentrate on our little venture. Right now, I could only concentrate on one thing.

"I expect you to make me proud," Callum's words kept *playing in my head.*

I needed to show him that he was right to trust me. But most importantly, I had to prove to myself that I deserved my place in the Realm, something I failed to do back on Earth.

Chapter Ten

Currently, Jake is laughing at me. Why? Well, because I told him that I thought food appeared by magic in the Realm. We were in the kitchen, a place where most people around here do not usually visit. However, Jake, being quite an exception makes it a habit of sneaking in there very often, to the extent of befriending the chefs. The best part is that to my amusement, the chefs here are Elves!

In the fairytales I read before coming here, Elves were either small and mean creatures or tall and courageous beings. From what I saw, I would say that their sizes vary, just like for humans. One thing which was real from fairy tales though, was the ears. They were pointy to enable better hearing. Their humour was what I enjoyed the most, even though their agility and their magic never ceased to surprise me. Jake explained that elves love to serve the chosen ones as a means to feel closer to the Divine.

Jake was stuffing his mouth with apple pies while I enjoyed having a culinary discussion with an elf.

"The secret behind these apple pies is that most of the batter consists of lemon peelings and cherry," Trevor explained.

"But why is it called apple pies then?" I asked, obviously confused by this information.

"Apple pies were invented by elves. Light years ago, our ancestors found it difficult to differentiate between apples and cherries, since in the Realm, cherries are as big and they grow together with apples. So, the recipe was made of both and they named it apple pie."

At times, it was hard to differentiate between what was real and what was a joke with the elves. But Trevor said that he would teach me how to make an apple pie. I will really know the recipe then.

"Jake, Aine, come here," Masha, an old lady elf called us.

I joined her behind the counter while Jake swallowed the remaining apple pies and jogged to us.

"I heard that you are going for training at the Edge. Take this with you." She handed us a bottle of water and a sack of fruit each. "The coconut water will help you rid of tiredness faster than usual while the sack of dried berries will give you extra energy. Eat them before going and bring the coconut water with you."

We thanked Trevor and Masha, and after promising to visit again soon, we left to prepare for our special training. Jake and I parted ways on reaching the dorms as our rooms were in different corridors. Before going to my room, I decided to drop by to Samhain's room since we did not have time to talk much lately.

After knocking twice, the door opened and I saw Samhain collecting his arrows from the target in his room.

"Hi," I said, entering his room. My eyes could not ignore the dirty pile of clothes present on his floor. '*Typical boy,*' I thought.

"Hey Aine," he greeted, "What brings you to my modest dwelling?"

"I was just visiting," I said, "We did not get to exchange many words since our arrival here."

"Yeah, that's true," he said, "But," he added, "Would we not meet at training later anyway?"

"No, I won't be there. I got taken as a shooter and we have additional practice later."

"Oh!" He said as if acknowledging the words. "Well then, I guess you need to prepare. Do great there! And thanks for checking on your first friend here. I'll see you later Aine."

After my brief conversation with Samhain, I entered my room and took a quick shower before getting my bag ready. I set my daggers in place and did another piece of reading from my new book, hoping that I would find something useful again.

When it was close to one o'clock, I made my way to the Shooters' training room, eating my dried berries on the way. While waiting for everyone else to come, Jake included, I made a conversation with Maxwell and Myron, two twins who I felt would become my guy best friends. From the stories they told me, they had been here for the past week and still complain about not having a twin room. They were allocated to separate rooms each but unhappy about that decision, they would take turns to bring their beddings to the other's room and spend the night on the other's floor occasionally.

Soon after, every shooter entered the room. Jake was the last to enter. He came to stand where I was standing with Maxwell and Myron while Damien, the chief instructor for shooters silenced the whole room.

"We will leave for the Edge soon," Damien started, "You all need to listen to instructions or the Demon's saliva will burn you to death. Remember what you were taught and use the strategies you think are best."

After explaining the rules for one last time, we walked past the garden of Elixir, to a clearing which was thirty minutes away. Then, because walking to the Edge would take more than a day, Jordan, another Elite warrior, opened a Portal which would minimize the traveling time by twenty- four hours.

The portal however, was not made of magic but of very advanced technology; technology I did not understand yet. Jordan placed two small metal devices on dried land and turned to face us.

"These devices are called Captors. Once activated, they will only last for five minutes. I suggest you get in a queue now and once we give the signal, you have to walk straight through it." He explained.

After pressing on several buttons on the captors, Jordan pressed a code on a remote control kind of device he had and one by one, everyone started going through the virtual looking blue wall.

Jake was right in front of me and I was followed by Myron. I watched Jake walk through the portal and when he was gone, I walked to it and stepped in.

The teleportation though was not as smooth as expected, literally. The second portal though was set a bit further from the Edge, in another clearing. However, they put it on a slope making it logical that anyone stepping through for the first time would lose their balance and land on their bum. Being no exception, I stumbled forward and as Jake was trying to stand back up, I hit him in my fall, knocking him down.

"I'm so sorry!" I exclaimed, ashamed. I could feel my cheek heating up and I tried not to think about others seeing the blush on my face.

"It's okay!" Jake said laughing and rubbing his back at the same time.

I on the other hand did not get hurt due to Jake being my safety cushion during the fall. After standing up, Jake pulled me up quickly in order not to get smashed by the other two boys falling in an avalanche.

When all ten of us shooters were finally standing, we watched as Damien, followed by Jordan came through the portal, stepping perfectly on the ground as if expecting the slope. They were laughing their heads off as they walked down to where we were standing.

On reading the confused expression on our faces, they both stopped laughing.

"What?" Damien asked, grinning. "Who said we were not allowed to pull a joke during a crisis!"

After our instructors were done with their little joke, it was time to get back to being serious. After another fifteen minutes of walking, we reached the famous Edge they were talking about.

"Behind those barriers," Damien started explaining pointing towards the huge metal walls, "Is what we call the Edge. Few months ago, the demons successfully casted a portal made from dark magic, creating a passage from the demonic land to the Realm of Angels and Spirits. We have not been able to shut it, so, a group of warriors is posted here every day.

These metal barriers are made of a technology created to resist demons, but we believe they are not invincible. The demons which keep coming behind these walls are extremely dangerous and usually killed on sight. However, for your training, you will be facing these creatures alone, applying the knowledge and strategies we shared as well as your own talents. Level two Elite Warriors will only intervene in case of extreme emergency. Any questions?"

A shooter named West was the first to speak.

"How long are we supposed to be there?"

"You will fight for one hour since the demon always keep coming, after one hour of training we will interfere and cover for you while you exit the clearing." Jordan answered.

As we were getting closer to the barrier, another Elite Warrior stopped Damien.

"Are you sure they are ready to face this?" he asked looking in our direction.

"Tyler, trust me," Damien answered. "They are stronger than we all were on our first year. Besides, we don't have a choice. Callum said we could not afford wasting more time. Everything is happening under his orders!"

After talking to Damien, Tyler signaled the other warriors. They made a passage through the clearing and soon after, we were told to leave all our belongings outside. Carrying only our weapons, we entered the now opened clearing. On feeling our presence, the demons started screeching and the shooting begun. Moving forward and shooting the demons' heart, I was close enough to see the portal through which demons entered.

For some demons however, shooting was of no use for they had no hearts. We had to improvise and find strategies to use their own poison against them. Moving around to trap the demons, we made them spit their acidic saliva on their fellow demons. However, being only ten shooters for hundreds of demons was not very effective. As we killed the demons, others kept entering through the portal.

I was getting to the middle, closer to the portal and my plan to make them kill each other was working just fine. Unfortunately, I had already lost two of my precious daggers. I was about to shoot a Dramoniagus when a demon with over ten tentacles hit my hand with its thorn filled tentacle, cutting deep along my skin and sending my dagger flying. My dissatisfaction was soon overlooked when the flying dagger hit another Dramoniagus in the heart, bursting it open. The only misfortune was that I would not be able to use my right hand soon but luckily for me, I was not that bad left handed. With an agility I never noticed before, I quickly reached for my left ankle and took another of the spare daggers. Knowing that my friend in front had no heart it would be harder to hit it, but making use of my speed, I ran fast enough and shot the demon in the eye instead. The creature fell unconscious to the ground but knowing that it would wake up in no time, I hurried on top of it and pulled my dagger out.

I turned around and saw a Dramoniagus preparing to spit its acidic content on me. Fortunately, Dramoniagus were quite slow in spitting, giving me enough time to go behind it and shoot it in the heart. However, I was too close and the gross black liquid from the Dramoniagus landed on me after the explosion. Some drops of the acidic content from the heart of the Dramoniagus burnt my skin but hopefully, it was too few to empoison, or even kill me.

I started to worry when I could see none of the other warriors from where I was and instead, I found myself surrounded by a bunch of demonic creatures. I reached down to take another dagger when I realized that I had none left. Being in the middle of so many demons with a temporarily disabled right hand and no weapons was no good sign. I saw the demons encircling me, moving closer. There was no escape. Frightened and on instinct, my first reaction was to crouch down to protect myself. But I knew that there was nothing I could do save myself. I had never seen a demon kill before. I wondered what it would do to me. Whether they would eat me or burn me with their acidic saliva, death was surely certain.

As I expected the pain, I heard a voice in my head. Callum.

"Aine," he said, *"I expect you to make me proud."*

I could not die again. I could not let a bunch of stupid brainless demons kill me again. I thought about all those I found on coming to the Realm. I remembered the trust Callum and Sam had in me. I remembered the promise I made to Trevor and Masha of visiting again soon. I had to survive. I had to win this.

The strong desire I felt to survive caused a bubble of heat to explode in me. I felt the heat travel from my heart.

'*I need to live,*' I kept repeating.

Seconds later I felt the heat immerse from my body and my crystal felt cold on my neck. Still closing my eyes, I stood up and let determination take over me. I let the heat from within take over my whole body as it burned through the air. I heard the demons screech and it made me feel satisfied. Demons have been the cause of suffering on Earth and everywhere else.

Those disgusting creatures always tried to bring bad influence wherever they went and it was high time they pay.

When the noise died down, I open my eyes, feeling accomplished. Then, looking around me, I realized what I just did. The creatures had been replaced by piles of ashes. I stood in the middle of the clearing while the remaining warriors remained scattered away from me, looking shocked.

I looked at my hands; scorching red from the fire I caused. I was starting to feel scared of what I did. Everyone would probably think I'm dangerous and a threat. I did something I had only imagined possible in fictional stories. I felt the heat of my body die down as my skin took its normal colour. Luckily, I was not standing completely nude because the burnt fabric from my fabric had covered my body in carbon layers.

I saw Jake approaching me. He removed his T- shirt and handed it to me. I put it on. It looked like a mini dress on me but considering the situation, it was awesome. Then, in a very gentleman like manner, he saluted me, going down on one knee. His gesture was soon followed by all the other warriors.

"You are the fire," I heard a female voice in my head.

Chapter Eleven

I only spent the past three weeks in the presence of the Elders. Callum then took the time to explain that he knew who I was from the beginning but coming out as 'The Daughter of Fire' was all up to me. In those three weeks, they taught me all they knew about *my previous incarnations*. The whole concept still felt weird to me. I was told that I go back to Earth after my mission is over and take birth as a new individual, until I am needed to serve again. My last incarnation as The Daughter of Fire goes back to three hundred light years.

Knowing perfectly that I needed time to go through all the information I received about myself, Callum allowed me to regain my room. Or rather, because during the past week, I started taking full control over my new found ability and I needed to get ready for the ceremony. Something I really enjoyed though was what I called the 'Teleportation on the go.' Sure, being the Daughter of Fire came with lots of risks and responsibilities but it also had its advantages. Since I was not ready to face anybody yet, teleporting from the elders' chambers to my room was a lot easier.

I was back in my room to notice the dress I agreed on wearing for the ceremony and the matching pair of chic sneakers. Dahlia, one of the lady elders thought that it would be most appropriate to wear a red gown with heals. But thanks to my debating skills, I managed to convince her to let me wear a simple and chic back dress with its matching sneakers, which by the way come from the usual stores on Earth.

I was getting ready for the ceremony after shower, pausing occasionally to let my thoughts take over me. I'll agree; I have been feeling lonely and scared for the past weeks. I did not meet or talk to my friends because I was too afraid to know what they would think about me, now that I am different.

After putting my dress and the shoes on, I looked at myself in the mirror. I can't guess if my appearance changed from being here. I let my hair fall back on my shoulders from my towel. I always preferred letting my curly hair dry naturally for special occasions. Then, my eyes landed on my now red crystal. I really loved the colour even though I missed the black one. It felt strange being the Daughter of Fire. I looked at my reflection one last time before going to adjust my new set of daggers. However, I was grateful that makeup was not a custom in the Realm.

The cool thing about my dress was that it had secret compartments for my daggers. My new set was similar to the last one except for the runes engravings on the blade. Given my gift for casting runes, the runes on my daggers would allow me to summon them in times of need.

Feeling that there was nothing missing, I started reading the new books given by Philip until it was finally time for me to be at the ceremony.

I heard a knock on my door. Thinking that it would be Dahlia to check if I looked presentable, I opened the door and still looking at my book I said,

"Dahlia! I told you to trust me. See, I put on the dress and my hair is also lady like!"

"You look amazing!" I heard a male voice behind me.

Shocked, I stood up and turned to face my visitor.

"Jake?" I asked, certainly not expecting to see him.

"Hello to you too, Aine!" He said smiling. He was looking more of a smart guy than a warrior in his black tuxedo.

"Hi," I said shyly, "I was not expecting to see you here," I admitted.

"Waiting for someone else?" He asked, looking kind of sad for a while.

"No one actually," I said, "It's just that, I have not been meeting many people recently," I confessed.

"Not even your friends?" He asked looking concerned.

"No," I simply said.

"And may I ask why?"

"It's just that," I started, "I don't know! I guess I'm just scared."

"You! The strongest warrior here, Daughter of Fire, you are scared?" He asked not believing it.

"Back on Earth, I was a bit different from my friends. I would dream of and think differently than the rest and it always made me feel apart and alone. On coming here, I thought that it would be different because everyone seems to be equal. But recently, things did not exactly go as expected!" I said, feeling the tears run down my cheeks as I spoke.

"Aine," Jake said, wiping my tears. "How things turn out to be depend entirely on us. It only occurs if we allow it to. You need to face the situation and talk to your friends. If you keep hiding from the situation, it will only deteriorate and it will certainly not make you happy. Do you understand what I mean?"

My only respond was to nod understandingly.

Then, as if to cheer up the situation, Jake said,

"Well today is your day! How about we go to that party that is being held in your honour?" He asked, giving me his hand to hold.

I took it and together we walked back to the Court Room where the ceremony was being held.

Knowing that I was not ready to face everyone at once yet, Jake took another less used pathway.

Once we were inside, Jake released my hand and we were immediately surrounded by many warriors greeting me. I said 'hello' and continued moving forward until I found my friends. Kerah was the first to show her affections. I was soon trapped in her embrace as she told me how much they missed me. She made me promise that I would talk about all of this later before releasing me. Then, I hug Samhain and Thomas. When I asked for the others, they told me that they had been tempted by the banquet and got lost there instead. I laughed at the information, clearly recognizing my hungry friends.

"May I please have your attention?" Philip asked.

All noise died down as everyone turned to look at the Elder warrior speaking.

"Aine, can you please come up here?" He said referring to stage where they were currently standing.

Jake nodded at me encouragingly and I made my way to join them.

Once I was up, Philip continued,

"After over three hundred light years, we are blessed to be in the presence of the Daughter of Fire again. We have been waiting for Aine to discover her inner self for a long time and gladly, it did not take much longer. I know that many of you are hungry and others mostly want to enjoy. We won't bore you for much longer. Let us begin the ceremony."

Callum walked next to us holding a tall red candle.

"According to the traditions which started ever since the first Daughter of Fire appeared," Callum started, looking at me. "Aine, Daughter of Fire, do you promise to serve the Realm of Angels and Spirit, the Devine and fight the evil to accomplish the purpose of your holy presence? If so, light this candle here, symbolizing that your flame will watch out for our people."

Just then, Philip approached me and whispered, "You know what to do!"

Shocked, I look at him wondering how he knew I did this before but then I smiled at his humour.

I took out my dagger and carved the fire rune on the red candle. Then, remembering the incantation, I pinched the top of the candle, just like I did before and whispered, "*Circa aërem ignis a me da mihi.*" Then, I replaced my hold of the candle with a flame dancing on its top.

"Daughter of Fire," Callum spoke. "We are honoured to have you among us."

The sound of clapping echoed around the room and right then, classical music was heard.

The warriors around us started dancing with their partners while I made my way to my friends. I was about to join them when Jake appeared in front of me.

"May I have a dance with the Daughter of Fire?" He asked, offering me to hold his hand.

I grabbed it and he brought me to the middle of all those dancing. I saw Kerah grinning at me. Her look told me that she was going to tease me about this forever.

"I like your style!" Jake said looking at my shoes and smirking.

"I cannot handle high heels!" I admitted.

I danced with Jake, following the beats until the music was over. I was about to join my friends at the banquet when we heard the sound of a window shattering. Seconds later, we saw an arrow go through the crowd while girls screamed. Someone was definitely hurt but I did not see who yet. I teleported to where the attack was held and I saw Philip lying on the floor in a puddle of blood, his white suit soaked in red.

Callum immediately shouted, "He is not dead, but he needs help now."

Then, he pulled the arrow from his shoulder, he smelled it and said, "Demons' acid! Quick!"

Some guides helped Callum carry Philip to the infirmary. Elite warriors started running around the place looking for the attacker.

"So it's true! The Daughter of Fire is back!"

Everybody turned to look at the speaker. A tall man, dressed in leather pants and a ripped black T- shirt spoke. He had long black hair, which was turned into corn rows., He was lying on his back at the top of a table on the stage.

"Who are you?" I asked, clearly showing my lack of affection for the attacker.

Right then, three elite warriors ran in his direction preparing to shoot. Expecting the attack, he faced them and with a swipe of his hand, he sent all three warriors flying to the other side of the room. "I would not try to do anything stupid if I were you" he said looking at everyone.

Then, turning to face me, he said, "You can ask about my details with your elders later. Just tell them Darion came!"

"What do you want?" I asked, not in the mood for his dark humour.

"That's more like it!" he said. "You see, is something you need from me and I have a price for that!"

"What do you mean?" I asked, confused.

"Well, your poor Philip is in a very bad condition right now." He paused. Approaching me, he continued, "But, it's nothing to worry about. At least, not yet. There is nothing your healers can do to cure him! But, I have the antidote. To get that, you will need to do something for me. I will come to take you in two days," he said, stopping in front of me, "If you refuse, he dies! If you take too much time, he will die in one week anyway."

"What is it you need from Aine?" Jake asked, standing next to me.

Ignoring Jakes presence, Darion faced me. He came closer to my right ear and whispered, "Don't do anything foolish, I'll see you in two days." Right then, he kissed my cheek and disappeared in some kind of black smoke.

I stood still looking at the empty space where Darion stood seconds ago. I felt like I was at a at a cliff-hanger. It was time for me to do something as the Daughter of Fire. Philip needed to be saved. Yet, I was unsure of what to do; should I really do what he wants? I did not know.

I needed to act fast and this time, no mistakes would be allowed!

Chapter Twelve

It pained me to see Philip lying in that infirmary bed, vulnerable. He had always been a father like figure to me. I remembered my first day on opening the Temple door; he greeted and initiated Samhain and I. remembered how he had been supporting me, especially when I was feeling alone due to discovering that I was the Daughter of Fire. It also made me feel guilty. Last night, Darion had come and upset the whole atmosphere and here I am, the Daughter of Fire, as they call me, feeling useless for not knowing what to do. I kissed Philip on his forehead, promising to be back again and I exited the infirmary.

Ever since last night, Callum had spent his whole time in the board room. I needed to act fast and for that, I needed to know more about Darion. I opened the board room's door and started addressing to Callum,

"Callum," I started angrily, "We cannot afford to lose any more time!"

I did not know why he has been keeping me in the dark. I had no idea why he would ignore me whenever I asked about Darion. Whatever it is, I had to know. If anything, I needed to know how to save Philip.

"Aine!" he said, "Listen," he started.

"No! You need to tell me everything you know about this. I need to know. Philip is there dying slowly on that god damn bed. If there is anything I can do to stop that, I will do it. I promised to do it. We need to stop that psycho of Darion."

Callum did not say anything. He went into another sub room of the board room. I followed him there and the door closed. I looked around, it was an office filled with books and lots of papers.

"Darion used to be one of us. We were in the same batch. He was one of the best. He had a gift for discoveries and science. We were working on a weapon to exterminate demons. We began experimenting with a Dramoniagus body. We were trying to make a sort of weapon that would destroy thousands of demons. But," he paused and looked outside the window.

I approached him. "But?" I asked.

"But an accident occurred." He continued.

"What accident?" I said putting my hand on his shoulder to encourage him.

"He accidently cut his own hand and the demon blood entered his system. We tried to remove it but we could not and he said he was fine. The experiments continued normally for some months. One day, he was caught drinking demon blood. We tried to talk to him, thinking the demon's blood clouded his mind. But instead, he tried to convince us to do the same. He said that it made him stronger and better. This matter was reported to the higher council and after evaluation it was decided that he would start a treatment and he would always remain under supervision."

"And what happened?"

"One day before starting the treatment, he made a portal to the demonic land. Many of those present tried to stop him but he killed them. We never saw him ever since."

"But, if he is back now, what do you think he wants?" I asked remembering he said I would need to do something if I want the antidote.

"For over twenty years, he must have continued with the experiments. But his intentions are bad and his magic is black. If he needs you, there must be something he wants to achieve, something bad that he cannot do without your magic."

Suddenly, there was a knock on the door and Sam entered holding a flask of dark green liquid.

"Callum," he said moving forward. "We did as you said and analyzed the poison basing ourselves on The Jeremiah exploration journals."

"And?" Callum asked looking hopeful.

"The substance they inflicted to Philip is made from a mixture of demon blood and Gladsome leaves. According to the Jeremiah exploration journals, it is the most common used poison in the demonic land." Sam said.

"Can it be cured?" Callum asked.

"Yes, there is only one way to cure it, we need to make him swallow the boiled juice of the black daisies' petals." Sam answered looking worried.

"Okay!" I said. "Where do we get those black daisies' petals?" I asked.

"According to the Jeremiah Journals, the black daisies only grow on a mountain in the Demonic land."

"Who is Jeremiah by the way?" I asked.

"Jeremiah was blessed like you. He looked very much like an angel; or that's just because of the feather wings. But unlike you he has the power of ice."

"So, he is the son of ice?"

As soon as the words left my mouth, Sam started laughing loudly.

"What?" I asked.

"Aine," Callum was the one to spoke. "Just being blessed does not mean that the blessed one becomes the Son or the Daughter of the power they have. Fire is considered as a mother. So a blessed red one with the power of summoning fire is considered the Daughter of Fire. Jeremiah however was blessed by an angel to serve."

"But what happened to him?"

"Jeremiah was sent to explore the demonic land light years ago. He served the Realm for many years and occasionally explored the demonic land and made us maps and other journals to inform us about everything. However, something happened, something we don't know about and one day, he did not come back. He sent his journals but we did not hear anything about him since then. There is a possibility he was killed."

"If Jeremiah found a way to the demonic land for his explorations, there's a possibility it can be done again and we can get the black daisies' petals for Philip, right?" Sam asked.

"Yes, that's right!" I answered. "Callum, can we use the already opened portal the demons used?"

"No, going through a demonic portal would kill any other traveller and warn the demons." Callum said. "But," he added, "There is another way!"

Callum opened a drawer at the desk. He took out a black rolled fabric. He unwrapped its content to reveal a handful of dark purple crystals and a flack filled with black grass.

"I will start the ritual to cast the crystals. In the meanwhile, Sam will explain everything you need to know and he will help you get ready. Now hurry!" Callum said before exiting the room with the materials in his hand.

"Aine, come with me." Sam said exiting the room too.

Following Sam outside the board room, I could only hope Callum's plan would work. This whole situation was not about me fitting in anymore! Philip's survival depended on the success of this mission.

"*My daughter,*" I heard the voice again. "*You are ready! You can do this.*"

Chapter Thirteen

We were going back to the court room where Callum would be casting the portal. Sam explained everything I needed to know. The black daisies were very rare but luckily, I'd be able to get some on the mountain after crossing the forest I'll be landing in. We entered the court room to see Callum with my friends organizing the crystals.

Jake looked at me, looking worried but did not say anything.

"Aine!" Kerah called running towards me. "Can we accompany you?"

Before I could answer, Callum spoke, "My child, this is a dangerous mission and the fewer they are, the fewer the chances to notice her presence."

Kerah nodded understandingly. Then Callum turned to face me.

"However, you need to be very careful. Kill any demon which notices you! Else they would report to their leaders."

"Their leaders?" I asked.

"You mean like Satan or Lucifer?" Thomas questioned.

"No, those beings do not reside in this world. However, there are fallen warriors, others who have been corrupted just like Darion!"

After everything was ready, I took my bag and got ready for my jump through the portal.

Spreading the herbs around it, Callum whispered some more words we could not understand. When he was done, he looked at me and said,

"The portal will only last for ten seconds after it appears. Remember, to come back, you need to visualize the portal and your return."

He took the remaining grass in his hands and blew it in the direction of the aligned crystals. A green translucent hole appeared inside the circle of crystals.

I looked at it preparing to jump.

"We will be waiting for your return, Daughter of Fire." Callum said.

And I jumped.

Chapter Fourteen

I woke up in the middle of what seemed to be burnt grass in a forest. I don't exactly know what happened inside the portal. But, I guess it went fine, considering my whole body was in one piece and I still had my backpack. I stood up looking around me to spot any unwanted visitors, but hopefully, there were none.

I took the journal out and looked at the map Jeremiah had drawn. Sam said that I was supposed to land exactly at the same spot he did ages ago because the grass came from that specific place. I checked on the map. Jeremiah had indicated a tree with a bird sign engraved on it.

More trees had grown in the past few hundreds of light years ever since Jeremiah had drawn this map. I spent quite some time analyzing the trunks to find the bird engraving. On the fourteenth tree, I found a symbol on the tree looking quite like a bird. I used my dagger to shape it more, in case of future explorations. Once I found the marked tree, my way was going to be easier.

For hours, I kept walking towards the north. The mountain was supposed to be in that direction. Jeremiah forgot to mention it was a huge forest. On my way to the mountain, I saw some Dramoniagus. One dagger to the heart of each and they were gone. My new daggers were invincible. The runes casted on them allowed them to be stronger than normal ones.

When night started to fall, I took it as a hint to rest. Since I was on my own, I figured out that spending the night at the top of a tree would be less risky to prevent any demons from killing me in my sleep. But, remaining on my guards did not help with falling asleep. I spent most of the night looking out for any possibility of danger. At every sound, I would grab my dagger and wait for the offender to show itself until realizing that it was only the wind rustling.

I woke up in the morning, on top of my tree, to find a bunch of demons going around the place. There were too many to be killed with my daggers and using my fire would only alert every creature around. Swiftly, I descended the tree and silently made my way around the area, until I could find no demons around. I kept walking, hoping that somehow, Jeremiah's journal would bring me to that mountain.

By midday, I reached what seemed to be the foot of a gigantic mountain. I put the journal back in my bag and started ascending it, hoping that I would find the black daisies somewhere. As I walked, the forest got denser and light seemed to be scarce. Casting a little fire in my right hand, I continued walking.

However, it was not encouraging to walk with no sign of the flower. I still had the drawing Sam showed me of the flower. But, there was no sign of any flowers at all!

"Maybe it was a long time ago and the flower stopped growing," I wondered.

I had to do it for Philip. Everyone at the Realm was counting on me.

With my goal in head, I kept walking and looking for the flower.

"You are very close!" I heard the voice again.

I wondered who that woman was. I heard her voice every time something major occurred. But, right now, I had no time to solve riddles. I kept moving forward and looking around the forest, analyzing every single leaves in case the flower was smaller than what I thought.

Suddenly, at the foot of a tree, I found it. Three black daisies were right in front of me. I kneeled on the floor to pluck them and put them in a flask before shoving it in my bag. Closing my bag, I visualized the portal and my strong desire to go back to the realm. Seconds later the portal appeared in front of me.

I went to stand closer to it for my jump. As I tried to leap over it, I felt a hard echo under my feet. I was so close to ending my mission when the floor beneath my feet collapsed. I slipped into what seemed to be a cave while the portal disappeared into thin air.

I stood up and saw what seemed to be a lab. On a rusted iron table were several flasks of different colored liquid. I kept walking around the place until in a corner I found what seemed to be bars forming a door. It was so dark inside that I could not figure out who the prisoner was. I lit a small fire again and used its dim light to look inside. There, in a corner, seemed to be a boy, looking slightly older than me. His right leg was chained and his clothes torn. He was lying unconscious on the floor and there was something covering him. I looked again closer and saw a pair of white feathered wings.

"Jeremiah!" I exclaimed loudly, shocked.

"Ah! Look who found her friend," I heard Darion's sadistic voice behind me.

Chapter Fifteen

I opened my eyes to find somebody sitting cross legged next to me. His hand was pressed to my forehead while he was whispering some words I could not understand. His large wings neatly spread behind him shielded my eyes from the light.

I stood abruptly and exclaimed loudly again, "Jeremiah!"

He looked at me with warning eyes and I heard his voice in my head.

"Don't talk loudly," he said. *"They might hear us."* He *looked towards a door from where we could hear some loud voices.*

Focusing on him, I thought, *"They?"*

"Darion and all the rest like him. The corrupted children! They were the ones to lock us for years and practice dark magic."

"Us?" *I asked whispering this time.*

"Mother and me. We have been here for so long. She is weak. They have been draining her energy."

"Who is she?" I asked.

He pointed to a far off corner. Adjusting my eyes to the dim light, I focused on the area. There, chained to large a pillar was a lady. Dark marks appeared where the chains were pressing on her skin. She looked defeated and bruised. I could not see her face properly as her tall black and silky hair fell in front of her. The wings were like Jeremiah's; white and majestic. He white dress had been torn and dirtied. I noticed some tubes connected to various places on her body, draining a silvery liquid from her. Suddenly, my eyes landed on a symbol on her arm where the sleeve had be torn.

The angelic symbol!

The images started coming back to me.

From my memories, I saw her. Mother! We lived in the angelic sphere and demons had been poisoning the world. She had called us from our lectures. Jeremiah, my elder brother had been training to become as a fully initiated angel. He was just like father. He was strong with the same blond features. He had all the traits and qualities of a warrior.

On the other side, I was just like mother. I had the curly black hair and the soft features. Mother always praised the wisdom I had. She said it was rare for people my age.

Then, the time came for big measures to be taken. The Realm of Angels and Spirit needed help. Bad times would come as the demon would continue infecting the blessed beings to enter the bad side.

Mother had said that being angels meant that we would do sacrifices to protect the people from anything bad. She said we needed to part but her blessings would always be with us.

I remembered the last time we saw mother and father. They hugged us one last time before sending us as souls to the human world.

"When the right time comes, you will fulfill your destinies. But for now, you need to learn about the humans."

Those were the last words she told us before sending us to the human world.

I looked at my mother and then at Jeremiah. My brother. Remembering how we used to be, I hugged him. We had been separated for so many light years.

"Jeremiah?" I asked. "Why didn't you try to get her and yourself out of here for so many years?"

"We had been locked with black magic," He started. "I tried everything but I could never open it. Mother said that I needed to pretend I was weak and useless. And as per her plan, they would not drain my magic. They do not really know who I am. But Mother," He said looking at our mother's drained figure. "They knew she is an angel and used her for their experimentations. They had been trying to make a weapon to destroy the Realm and the Sphere."

"What? But if they have that weapon, it means, we won't stand for long!" I exclaimed, worried.

"But they don't!" I heard my mother's voice.

"Mother!" We both said at the same time.

"How happy I am to see both of my children together!" She said smiling.

We heard the door open. My mother went back to her defeated position while Jeremiah lied on the floor looking unconscious.

"Aine! The Daughter of Fire! How does it feel to be useless next to your even more useless partner?" Darion asked laughing.

"Play along!" I heard my brother's voice in my head.

Understanding the whole situation, I shouted desperately,

"What did you do to Jeremiah?"

"Oh, the poor soul! They used to call him their saviour. But look," he exclaimed motioning towards Jeremiah, "A little black magic, and he is as useless as a human being."

"Or, that's what he thinks!" I heard my brother say in my mind.

"And since there is no escape for you as well, I suggest you sit quietly while I create the weapon which will destroy your kind."

Taking a flask of the silvery liquid he extracted from Mother, he said, "And one last thing, don't lose your time praying to your dearest angels, they can't even save themselves. Look, another useless creature there!" he motioned towards Mother. "But unlike your friend, her blood will be precious to me."

Darion laughed and turned back to the liquids on the table. He begun mixing other liquids to Mother's blood.

"My children!" I heard Mother's voice again. I looked at Jeremiah and found him looking towards Mother too. He heard her too. "Don't worry about what he tries. Angel's blood is only beautiful to selfish beings but it holds no power or clue. It's time you both get out of here. Alone, this spell cannot be broken but together you can be free."

I looked at Jeremiah and found him staring straight at me.

I remembered one day when we were very young and playing hide and seek in Father's chamber. We found a diary with many drawings in it. We were still very young and we did not know the power of runes by that time. On the last page was the rune for merging fire and ice.

"The strongest of all," Father had said.

I was about to concentrate and carve my part of the rune with my fire when Jeremiah stopped me.

"Aine," he whispered, "You need to melt the openings first, in case the others hear us."

Nodding understandingly, I concentrated on the metal doors. Slowly, I let my heat move to the doors. I closed my eyes until I felt the flames were hot enough and melted the metal, locking the doors.

Probably thinking his experiments were causing the heat, I saw Darion moving away from the liquids he was heating.

Then, concentrating in the metal barriers in front of us, I waited until Jeremiah had casted the Ice rune with his power in front of us and continued by casting the hot flames to form the fire rune on it.

Kneeling next to me, Jeremiah held my hand.

"Once you get out, I will use the remaining energy I have to cast a portal back to the Realm of Angels and Spirits. It will be enough to drain my energy and send my soul back to the Sphere. You need to hurry up. The Realm needs you both. Darker times are coming." We heard Mother's voice while she looked at us.

We nodded and holding hands, Jeremiah and I concentrated on our runes. I thought about my life back to when our family was complete and together at the sphere. But then, the memories of the demons came back and I remembered that they had been the reason behind the separations. I felt anger bubble up inside of me. I let the anger and the fire flow out of me while feeling the cold from my brother's ice.

I heard the sound of the metal shattering and falling on the floor. I opened my eyes and saw Darion's shocked expression.

He hadn't expected Jeremiah and my get together to be this destructive.

"If you think breaking the doors will be enough--," Darion started but was stopped by Jeremiah.

"Enough! You unworthy soul," Jeremiah sounded angry and he had the right to be.

He walked in Darion's direction.

"Let me see what you can do to stop me!" Jeremiah challenged him.

He put his hand on Darion's shoulder and I saw Darion's horrified expression before he fell to the floor, looking scared.

"A little paralysis is not enough as a punishment for you for all your sins, but the suffering it will bring you is quite satisfying."

Darion tried to stand up by holding the table, but his legs failed to support him. Instead, he only managed to pull some flasks with him and what seemed to be Bunsen burners.

Some of the liquids fell on my bag which was close to Darion and suddenly, it caught fire along with the other liquids.

Watching the fire, I remembered the black daisies. Everyone had been counting on me to cure Philip. But it was too late. The black daisies had burnt along with my hope to cure Philip.

Looking at my bag which was only a pile of ashes, Darion laughed, probably knowing I had the only remedy for Philip in there.

"Aine, come on! We need to hurry," Jeremiah said.

Feeling defeated, I walked to my mother with Jeremiah.

I had found my brother and my mother, but this also meant I would lose Philip.

Concentrating back on our mother, we broke the chains holding her to that place.

"My children," she started, "How you've grown up! Seeing you after so long made me so happy. But the Realm still needs you. You need to go back for now. But, there is something else I need to give you before you leave."

She moved closer to the table where Darion was experimenting and took an empty flask. She closed her eyes and when she opened them, tears started flowing on her cheeks. She collected the tears in the flask and handed it to me.

"Angel's tears," she said, "The greatest remedy. It should be enough to cure Philip."

She handed the flask to me and I took it. Then, knowing it was goodbye, I hugged her one last time.

"I love you, Mother," I said holding her tight.

Jeremiah joined in our hug too. We then parted and she motioned us to make some steps away.

She joined her hands and closed her eyes concentrating. Seconds later, a bluish portal appeared in front of her and she opened her eyes.

She turned towards Jeremiah and I and said,

"It's time for every one of us to get back to duty. Remember, together, you can do great things!"

Just like that, she disappeared into thin air.

"We will meet again someday." We heard the voice echoing in the room.

Jeremiah took my hand in his and I followed him into the portal. Just before the portal closed, I felt something pierce through my back and heard Darion's laugh.

The portal closed and we got teleported back into the court room, right in the middle of the circle Callum had casted.

Right then, everyone started clapping and laughing on seeing me back. Suddenly, noticing Jeremiah, we heard whispers and they were followed by everyone bowing in our presence. I saw Jake looking reassured in a corner while Kerah, Thomas and Samhain laughed and hugged each other.

While the cheering continued, I felt dizziness take over me from the loss of blood. I lost my balance a bit, but still, I continued holding on to the flask my mother gave me. Callum approached us and feeling my consciousness drift away, I whispered,

"Bring me to Philip."

I felt my brother's support as he helped me stand up and Callum lead us to a room on the other side of the Temple. There, on a bed, we saw Philip lying down, unconscious. He looked like life was slowly drifting away from him. They brought me closer to him. Bringing the flask closer to his mouth, I emptied the content in his mouth. While praying that my mother's remedy would work, I felt my legs give out. Still bleeding, I felt the weight of my body knock me to the floor. The worried face of my brother, kneeling next to me, was the last thing I remember.

Epilogue

After one week of rest, I was fully recovered. My recovery did not take very long because the dagger Darion threw at me was my own and it was not infected. I was back into my room to get ready for tonight's celebration. A banquet was being held in honour of Philip's recovery, my success and Jeremiah's return. This time, Dahlia allowed me to wear whatever I wanted because this was a party and nothing formal. Since I did not get the time to prepare, due to lying in bed for a week, Kerah brought me a pair of slim jeans, knowing I would love the casual outfit. I paired it with a plain T- shirt and a pair of sneakers.

When I was ready, I made my way to the garden of Elixir, where the party was being held. I met my friends properly and excused myself when I saw my brother approaching. Kerah made some teasing comments which died down when I made the proper introductions.

"Jeremiah, these are my friends and guys, meet Jeremiah, my brother." I said smiling.

Their shocked expression was priceless but then, it became easier for them when they started noticing our resembling features.

Soon, the celebration started and warriors all around ate and danced happily. I noticed my brother engaging in what seemed to be a captivation conversation with Shanara, the level two guide whom Samhain and I first met on coming here.

Speaking of Samhain, I saw him in a far-off corner talking to Kelani, another level one archer. It had been long since we had a proper conversation, but, Samhain remained one of my best friends and as his best friend, I was going to tease him later on.

Excusing myself, I moved throughout the crowd and made my way to Jake. I had been spending a lot of time with him ever since I came back. And since I was in bed for a week, he had been the one to remain around all the time and help me.

"Jake," I said, tapping him on his shoulder.

"Aine, you are here! I've been waiting for you. Let's go."

Jake had promised to take me back to the kitchen because it had been a long time since I met Masha and Trevor and I planned on honouring my promise.

On entering the kitchen, I was greeted with hugs from Trevor and Masha.

"Our heroine is here!" Trevor exclaimed dancing around.

"How about you cut the cake to celebrate your comeback!" Masha approached me, holding a small cake. It was coated with white cream and pieces of strawberry was placed on top.

I cut the cake and Masha shared it among ourselves.

I ate a piece and I was soon hypnotized by the magical taste it held.

"It's amazing Masha!" I exclaimed eating my cake.

"You should be saying this to this young boy here!" Masha said motioning to Jake. "He came to see us every night because he wanted to learn baking, so that when you come back, he would surprise you."

I looked at Jake. He avoided my gaze and his face was completely red from blushing.

I thanked him and after eating, we said goodbye to the elves and walked back to the temple.

"Do you want to see something magical?" Jake asked.

"Yes, of course!" I said.

Leading the way, Jake brought me to a corner in the Realm and we took some stairs. We kept climbing them until we reached a door. I followed Jake as we walked on the top of the temple. Jake held his hand on my face, covering my eyes. We walked on the roof until he made me sit. When he removed his hands, I opened my eyes to see what seemed to be a garden with little butterflies-like creatures flying around.

Amazed by the sight in front of me, I pointed towards the tiny colorful creatures that looked like a fusion of humans and butterflies and asked,

"What are those?"

"Fairies." Jake said. "They are attracted to the smell of flowers."

Some of the fairies approached us and flew around us before going back to dancing around the flowers.

"Aine," Jake said. "There is something I need to tell you."

"Yes?" I asked.

"It will probably sound lame to you because you are cool, powerful and the daughter of fire, while I am a mere shooter but I started having feelings for you. It started when I first met you, when I saw you shoot that Dramoniagus to save me. Ever since, you kept surprising me and my feelings kept growing. I know that you probably won't feel the same because I am nothing. But, I just wanted to tell you about my feelings and..."

I silenced him by kissing him on his cheeks.

He looked at me, surprised.

"First, thank you!" I started. "If it was not for you, I would not have found the courage to face who I really am and do all that I did. You were the one who kept supporting me and that too, before I came out as the daughter of fire. So, don't you ever dare say that you are nothing compared to me because you really are an amazing and special person. I needed you then and I know that I would always need you to help me."

I stopped and looked at him, smiling.

"And the second thing?" he asked, smiling.

"And second," I said, "I like you too."

I could feel myself blushing. But, since it was Jake sitting in front of me, I felt a bubble of happiness growing in me, instead of being shy.

Jake pulled me in for a kiss and I felt genuinely loved after a long time.

I pulled away from the kiss and saw Jake looking at me, confused.

I looked at him and said,

"Just promise to always be by my side." I told him.

In a fraction of seconds, his expression changed from a confused one to that of a happy child on Christmas.

"I promise," he said, grinning, before pulling me in for a hug.